CW00515499

Chantecoq

Ladykiller

The Further Exploits of Chantecoq, Volume 8

Arthur Bernède

Translated by Andrew K. Lawston

DEDICATION

For Melanie, and for Buscemi, the Kitten of Detectives.

CONTENTS

ACKNOWLEDGMENTS

This book was translated from *Le Tueur des Femmes* by Arthur Bernède, first
published by Editions Jules Tallandier in 1929. The source text can be read
online in the original French at:
https://gallica.bnf.fr/ark:/12148/bpt6k936307s.

The cover design was by Rachel Lawston of www.lawstondesign.com.

A FEW WORDS TO READERS

Here is the final volume in the series that we've dedicated to Chantecoq's further exploits.

Not that our famous friend doesn't still have numerous tales up his sleeve; but, as he puts it himself, with his customary modesty, you must never test the public's patience by retaining its attention for too long on the same character. Instead let's leave some time before we pick up, if our readers show any such desire, with a new series of adventures in which the vanquisher of Belphégor and so many other bandits will be the main hero.

Of the tales Chantecoq revealed, this, which we saved for last, may be the most gripping of all.

Indeed, in addition to the merit of true originality, it attaches the rare quality of profound humanity.

It shows us both how far the perversity of a brain exasperated by evil demons may go, while at the same time it shows us the courage, intelligence, and skill of a man who uses his directives only for doing good.

We're about to live through some moments of anguish

and even dread, but also to enjoy many moments of enthusiasm, inspired by the legendary bravado and genial perspicacity of the greatest bloodhound of our modern age.

The events that we are relating are recent in nature, however, as you will see in the course of their development. If they haven't spread widely among the general public and if the press have made only rare and brief allusions to it, it's because the honour of too many families was at stake, and it was necessary to preserve that honour at all costs.

With the scruples that all writers have, to do no harm with imprudent phrases or double entendres, to individuals who should not be held responsible for the weaknesses of certain of their families, we were forced, as in our preceding volumes, not to distort the truth, but to give it an expression so that it's impossible to recognise those who were directly or indirectly involved in this most mysterious of cases.

We forbid ourselves absolutely from trying to write what has come to be known as the *roman à clef*, that's to say, in the course of which it's easy to recognise, beneath the transparency of a veil lifted up by the slightest breeze, the contemporary personalities who were the protagonists of the drama in question.

Such processes, we leave to others. It's not through scandal that we aim to reach the masses, but solely through the truth which is fit to utter, that's to say through general examples which are designed more to provoke thought than studies which are too specific and which even risk, when they don't take care, to appear defamatory, not only in the eyes of those who read them, but also in the mind of those who inspired them. We will content ourselves with affirming simply that *The Ladykiller* existed, as did his victims.

ARTHUR BERNEDE

1 THE KING OF DETECTIVES

Our readers, who already know Chantecoq through the various accounts that we have given them of his adventures, will forgive us if, in deference to those who are unfamiliar with them, we recall here that the greatest private detective in the world lived in a very pretty cottage on Avenue de Verzy, a road which leads to Avenue des Ternes.

This building, buried under greenery and surrounded by a small garden which, gilded by the June sun, benefited from a calm atmosphere troubled only by the tranquil chirping of sparrows.

As we wrote in the *Mystery of the Blue Train*, the first volume in this series, in this pretty corner of Paris, "You feel... a sense of liberation, of relaxation, of well-being, and, in your joy at having finally evaded a dangerous zone, you say to yourself, 'How good it must be to live here!'"

If one were to enter the great bloodhound's home, one would feel this impression of well-being grow. The house, whose interior architecture recalls that of one of those pretty Normandy cottages such as can be seen on the beaches of

Calvados and the English Channel, appeared, at first glance, endlessly comfortable and charming.

One enters a large airy hallway, from which several doors open, of which one leads directly to the detective's study.

We're going to sneak in there immediately, without being announced by the excellent Pierre Gautrais: loyal valet, former brother in arms, and the master here.

It's two o'clock in the afternoon. In this vast room, which more closely resembles, from its furnishing as much as by the *objets d'art* found there, an artist's workshop rather than a private detective's office, Chantecoq, while smoking his pipe, finishes savouring an excellent mocha, in the company of his son-in-law Jacques Bellegarde, the well-known reporter for the *Petit Parisien*, by his daughter, the blonde and delicious Colette, and by his secretary, young Météor, a skinny little fellow, with curious eyes, endlessly on the lookout, and who owes his nickname to his faculty for appearing and disappearing with a speed which verges on the prodigious.

Chantecoq, although he has almost reached the age of fifty, gives the impression of a man aged barely forty years. He listens with a slightly mysterious smile to his son-in-law, who is in the process of bringing him up to date with the latest exploits of the individual as terrifying as he is ghostlike, to whom the press and public have given the nickname of *The Ladykiller*.

For several weeks, indeed, Paris has lived in a state of real dread. Each day, several women are dying suddenly, either at home, or in the street, even while watching shows.

Doctors are unanimous in establishing the same cause of death: embolism. The victims are, a very curious detail, almost exclusively very young and very pretty ladies.

It's almost as though, in a less brutal, less savage, less

atrocious form, the famous story of Jack the Ripper, after terrorising London around forty years ago, is beginning again in modern Paris.

Jacques Bellegarde, who has taken up this case at once and who has published a series of resounding articles in his paper, has brought his father-in-law the terrible morning bulletin, the latest list of victims which was brought to him at noon by police headquarters.

This is the note which he is reading aloud:

1. *The Marquise de Lézardrieux, the young wife of the deputy of Ille-et-Rance, died last night during a ball held for the English Ambassador;*

2. *The beautiful Lise Destelle, the splendid socialite of the Comédie Française, succumbed during supper, in the presence of one of the most important figures in the Republic;*

3. *Madame Henriette Mauléon, wife of the under-secretary of Waters and Forestry, expired this morning, while walking in Bois de Boulogne;*

4. *Madame Juliette Arbois, wife of a great automotive industrialist, died just as she was preparing to take the wheel;*

5. *Madame Raymonde Lordier, wife of the owner of the large Quatre-Saisons shop, gave up her soul at the beginning of a tennis match;*

6. *Madame Riberti, wife of the director of the Franco-Italian bank, struck down in her car, just as she was going to lunch with some friends at Café de la Régence, Place du Théâtre-Français.*

And Bellegarde added, "There's a somewhat unusual review. If this continues, all the pretty wives in Paris will end up there, one after the other."

Collette cried out, "You're giving me shivers all down my spine."

Bellegarde said, "I believe you, my darling, have nothing to worry about."

"Why's that?"

"From the confidential information that I've received from the mouth of the chief of police, investigations into those women who have been lost in such a strange fashion, revealed that they had all committed what the Gospel calls the sin of adultery."

"Oh! In that case," cried Colette, with a flash of complete sincerity and love, "I'm completely reassured. If *The Ladykiller* has erected himself as the avenger of wronged husbands, I have nothing to fear from him."

"I'm sure," replied Bellegarde, "and that's why I'm completely relaxed."

Chantecoq, who had listened to his son-in-law with great attention, said, while keeping his eye on the spirals that the smoke from his pipe drew in the air, "What do the 'officials' think of it all?"

Bellegarde replied, "They're literally 'poisoned'. Headquarters launched its whole elite rank of inspectors on the trail of this mysterious assassin. Better than anyone, you know that there are a few proven aces among them."

Chantecoq declared, "I'm the first to give them their dues, and to recognise that perhaps never before has the Parisian police boasted leaders so remarkable and a staff so intelligent, courageous and devoted. But I also declare that this time they have a terrible game to play. From what you told me, my dear Jacques, the doctors are unanimous in acknowledging that the victims died from the same disease, that's to say from an embolism!"

14

"Correct."

Chantecoq, who seemed to have some rather advanced medical notions, replied, "So, what's an embolism? The great doctor Velpeau[1], as I recall, defined it as: 'Obliteration of the artery produced by a fibrous clot that the circulation has brought from a larger artery.' Anyway, there's no need to be a great scholar to know that this accident is a frequent consequence of any phlebitis or deep vein thrombosis that ought to have a fatal outcome; which is also observed in the course of cancerous illnesses; that, in other cases, asphyxia is complete, fatal, and that death occurs following hematosis, that's to say from the transformation of red blood into black blood through the action of oxygen from the air, introduced into the lungs.

"That's all I know on the subject. It's obviously a hasty summary. In order to treat it in a more precise fashion, I'd have to not only consult the numerous medical books that I have in my library, but also confer with those who are called the men of the art.

"In any case, there's one thing I believe to be certain, this phenomenon of embolism could very well be caused by a

[1] Alfred-Armand-Louis-Marie Velpeau (1795-1867). A legendary French surgeon and anatomist. To this day, you can get a "Velpeau bandage" to immobilise your arm against your chest. He believed that pain-free surgery was a fairy tale, and was extremely cautious about the advent of early anaesthetics like ether and chloroform. That sounds mad now, but bear in mind that anaesthetics encouraged many surgeons to embark on deeper, longer and more complex operations... which ended up killing more patients than they saved, through secondary infection. It's one of the great tragedies of medical history that antiseptics were developed only several miserable decades after anaesthetics.

poisoning of the blood."

"Therefore," Colette observed, "you conclude, father, that these poor women were drugged."

He who was called so rightly the king of detectives replied, "I'm convinced, and I'll even add that I'm sure it wasn't by means of a poison mixed in with their food, but by means of an injection whose composition is a lethal poison, which leaves no trace in the victim."

"That's incredibly interesting," replied Bellegarde, "and if you wanted to give me an interview on that subject for the *Petit Parisien...*"

"My dear Jacques," replied Chantecoq, "you know very well that I'm always anxious to help you out when I can; but, unfortunately, I've promised myself, even sworn, to maintain the most absolute silence on this case. First, because I make it a principle never to involve myself in something which is none of my business, and because I'd never want to hamper the work of the official police, or to be seen to be giving them the smallest rebuke or slightest piece of advice."

"I understand you perfectly," declared Bellegarde, "and I promise I'll be completely discreet. However, this is between us: permit me to observe that I have the impression you're not in complete agreement on the methodology used by those tasked with the mission of getting their hands on the *Ladykiller.*"

"My dear Jacques," replied Chantecoq while filling a fresh pipe, "I'll answer you quite frankly that I have no opinion on this subject. I've followed this case in the papers; I've had some unvarnished information from you, like that which you've just given me; but that's wholly insufficient for me to establish for myself a semblance of conviction and above all to inspire in me a system for research."

"And yet, boss," said Météor, who, up to now, had been quiet, "this is a case which would have been pretty interesting to tackle, and I'm astonished that, among the numerous husbands who have become widows in a fashion as tragic as it is unexpected, not one among them who thought to come to you to shed light on what, following the old formula, I'll call a shadowy affair."

Chantecoq gave an ironic smile. "Who said they haven't been coming to me?"

At those words, all three listeners' faces became sharply attentive. Chantecoq continued.

"Now I can tell you, as I've resolved not to occupy myself with this Ladykiller, it wasn't one husband, but at least ten who have come to ask me, even beg me, to seek out this frightful bandit or, perhaps, who knows, this madman, this maniac, who has long succeeded in evading the clutches of France's most skilled policemen and continues - I won't say under their beards, as it's no longer fashionable to wear them, but under their noses, almost under their very eyes - his dreadful series of massacres…

"Well! I refused. You want to know why, don't you? I'll tell you… first, because I always have my principle, with only very rare exceptions, to avoid any antagonism or rivalry with Police HQ agents. Moreover, I always preferred to consecrate my brain, my heart, my skills and my strength to the defence of an irreproachable cause. Now, as our dear Jacques said, all those women were, it appears, unfaithful spouses. I deplore that they received such cruel punishment, but in the end, that whole world, however highly-placed it might be, hardly interests me and I prefer to abstain from it."

"However," Colette objected, "as you put it, the punishment appears to be disproportionate to the fault, and

I've often heard it said you would confound the husband or wife who, to avenge themselves for the betrayal of one or the other, makes use of a revolver, a knife, or poison.

"How many times have you complained to me about the indulgence shown by Parisian juries towards so-called crimes of passion? That's why I believe it would be dangerous for society to allow this *Ladykiller* to continue his work and perhaps risk sacrificing an innocent."

Bellegarde replied, "I completely agree with Colette."

Chantecoq, whose face had assumed an expression of gravity which further added to the purity of his classical profile, responded slowly, "Ladies, especially when they have an exquisite heart and a fine mind as you do, my dear Colette, sometimes see quicker than men the consequences of things which escape us.

"It's true, as you said, this criminal or madman may commit an error. Who knows if he might not already have committed one? If I had proof of that, I wouldn't hesitate to declare it; perhaps then, without appearing to do so, without risking annoying anybody, of upsetting any sensibilities, I would decide to enter into the battle against this phantom, who could well transform some day into a true scourge, from which humanity would suffer.

"But until then, I prefer to remain in the position of an observer and, I won't hide it from you, in any case, I'm keenly interested to know how my colleagues in the police will go about untangling this enigma, which seems to me to be excessively difficult to decipher.

"I even believe the police have rarely been faced with such a complicated problem. For my part, I loyally acknowledge that, if I was charged with resolving it, I would be particularly perplexed."

"Oh! Boss!" protested Météor, "Permit me to contradict you, with all the respect I owe you. As you put it, you might be frustrated for a few moments, but I know your instincts. I'm convinced your embarrassment would be of short duration and you wouldn't take long to discover this Ladykiller. I won't say that you've done better than this, but you've done just as well and I, who know you well, without the slightest spirit of flattery, I affirm that with you it wouldn't take long."

"Météor's right," said Bellegarde. "I'll even add that you're the only detective capable of unmasking and arresting this wretch."

Chantecoq replied, "I'm very flattered by the high opinion you have of me…"

Colette hastened to add, "I wouldn't hasten to contradict it."

The detective, forcefully, intoned, "There's no point insisting; I gave my reasons and I can only repeat: to change my attitude, I'd need a new and completely extraordinary revelation."

Hardly had he spoken those words than there was a discreet tap at the door.

"Come in," said Chantecoq.

His valet appeared. He was carrying in one hand a platter on which lay a sealed envelope.

Chantecoq opened it, and took out a calling card. He read the few lines of handwriting scribbled with a febrile hand beneath the caller's name. Then he gasped, "That's strange!"

He thought for a few seconds in deep silence, because his daughter, his son-in-law and his secretary, as well as his valet, were all used to being quiet around him whenever his demeanour seemed to indicate they should.

The great bloodhound, a broad smile on his face, said, "My dear Colette, you too, my dear Jacques, I'm going to ask you to restore my liberty to me. An important visit... most unexpected."

"Father," replied the young woman, "we were about to take leave of you, Jacques and I. He to pass by his newspaper's office, where I'll meet him after some shopping in Paris."

"Then, my children," declared the king of detectives, "farewell and see you soon, I hope!"

He kissed his daughter tenderly, shook Bellegarde's hand cordially and led them both to the door of his study, saying, "Unless unforeseen circumstances prevent it, I'll ask you on Sunday if I might come and have lunch at your charming property in Saint-Germain."

"Father!" Colette exclaimed, "it will be a great pleasure."

Jacques Bellegarde added, "As it is every time you come to see us."

The young couple walked away with the alert pace of happy people.

Chantecoq returned to Météor and said to him, "Go and sit at your usual listening post, and I'd ask you to take particular care with the stenography you're about to take. The conversation I'm about to have with the person I'm preparing to receive promises to be very interesting."

"All right, boss," said Météor, who vanished behind a red velvet curtain which clearly separated the study from another room.

Turning then towards Pierre Gautrais, who, with an almost military bearing, was awaiting his master's orders, Chantecoq said simply, "Show in Monsieur Maurice Barrois!"

2 A FAMILY DRAMA

Gautrais made an about-turn on principle, which would certainly have won him congratulations from a drill sergeant, and he vanished to the hallway.

Chantecoq, once again, looked at the card with interest. Though he would have given the order to show in a person whose name he was reading for the first time, it could only be that the lines scribbled on the elegant card were of the greatest importance, or at least were exciting a very deep professional curiosity in him.

The door opened again, making way for a man of around thirty, dressed with great elegance, whose frank, open face, and distinguished features, could only inspire immediate sympathy.

Chantecoq, with his customary courtesy, said, indicating a chair placed opposite his desk, "Monsieur, you're welcome and do please take a seat."

The visitor sat down. His face revealed intense anxiety, at the same time as a truly painful emotion.

"Monsieur Chantecoq," he began, "if I have taken the

fast, breathless, slight Peter Davison?

liberty of coming to you without requesting a meeting with you, it's because I need to obtain from you quickly, very quickly, as soon as possible, more than advice, that is to say your complete support."

Chantecoq, impassive, listened to his guest, who soon continued.

"Monsieur, as I wrote on my card in a few words, this is a matter of saving the life of an innocent, or rather of a wretch who is my brother. He wants to kill himself and you alone, Monsieur Chantecoq, can prevent such a terrible catastrophe."

"Monsieur," replied Chantecoq, "although I have the honour of meeting you today for the first time, your personality as well as that of your brother are not completely unknown to me: you are in fact the sons of Monsieur Auguste Barrois, metallurgist."

"Indeed."

This affirmation appeared to make a favourable impression on the great detective, because he replied at once, "I've been in contact with your father for around eight years now, on the subject of a theft of stocks of which he was the victim."

"I remember very well," replied Maurice Barrois, and my father told me that, thanks to you, he was able to recover the full value that was stolen from him. It's precisely in memory of that eminent service you did him, which proves to what extent your celebrity is justified, that my father and I decided by joint accord to appeal for your assistance."

"It is granted in advance, monsieur," replied the detective. "I have, indeed, excellent memories of your father, and I would be very happy if I could be of service to him once again."

The young industrialist replied, "I expected no less from you, Monsieur Chantecoq, because I knew that, if you're the most cunning detective in the world, you're also the best man on Earth."

Chantecoq, who was modesty itself, made a vague gesture of protest, then he replied.

"Now, monsieur, I'm listening to you with the greatest attention. I attach several conditions to that, as always: the first is that you tell me not just the truth, but the full truth; the second, is that you respond without hesitation to any requests for additional information that I address to you; the third and final condition is that you engage yourself not to ask me any questions, not only during the meeting we're having now, but during the investigation to which I'll apply myself and the steps I'll take with a view to preventing your brother following up on his thoughts of suicide."

Maurice Barrois replied with conviction. "On my honour, I agree to these conditions, Monsieur Chantecoq."

"Then all is well," said Colette's father. "We can work in excellent conditions and I'm going to do the impossible in order that your brother abandons his plans completely.

"When I get something in my head, it's very difficult to make me let go of it; because I'm one of those who have the principle that believing in victory is almost enough to achieve it."

In a tone of cordial benevolence, Chantecoq added, "Now you have the floor, tell me what are the reasons that are pushing Monsieur Jacques Barrois to destroy himself."

Encouraged by that welcome, the great metallurgist's youngest son, whose businesses figured among the most important in France, replied at once.

"My brother, who is honour and loyalty itself, married,

two years ago, a young girl without any dowry or expectations, and who, although belonging to France's highest aristocracy, was going to be reduced to giving English lessons or working as a guide to American visitors to France."

"Her maiden name?" asked the king of detectives.

"Marie-Louise de Beaurevoir."

"Good, do please continue."

"My sister-in-law was and still is remarkably beautiful. Even yesterday, we believed her to be as virtuous and as attached to my brother as an honest woman can be towards the man that she loves and to whom she owes infinite gratitude.

"She was nothing of the sort. Marie-Louise, beneath her appearance of charm, honesty, feminine delicacy, was hiding an abominable soul. For some time, my brother and I had been receiving anonymous letters formally accusing her of adultery.

"Those letters, that we considered calumnies, inspired only disgust in us and we paid them no heed, so odiously unbelievable did they seem to us.

"Indeed, they went so far as to accuse Marie-Louise of having intimate relations with a vague dancer from some spa town, furnished with a criminal record, who openly wanted to be the kept man of several very chic Parisian ladies.

"Now, this morning I was at home, around eleven o'clock, when I saw my brother enter my office like a gust of wind. Half-crazed, he shouted, 'My poor friend, I'm desperate, the anonymous letters were telling the truth: my wife is the mistress of this Gomez Stardo; I just had proof of it as at home, in my house, under my roof, I surprised Marie-Louise in his arms.'

24

"And my poor Jacques added, 'I know what remains for me to do, I must blow my brains out.'

"And, mad with sorrow, his strength spent, his heart fit to burst, he fainted. Immediately I telephoned my father, who came running with a doctor. He diagnosed a simple fainting fit.

"My brother soon returned to his senses and, more and more overexcited, in the grip of a mad fever, again he shouted, 'I want to kill myself, I want to die!'

"The doctor succeeded, not without difficulty, to administer a sedative to him, thanks to which he could get a few hours' rest. I took the opportunity to visit my sister-in-law, who had gone out.

"Then, on my father's advice, I came to see you, to ask your advice. That's the whole truth, just as you asked me. Tell me now, Monsieur Chantecoq, what you can do to prevent the catastrophe I feel looming over us."

Chantecoq replied. "This case is outside the field in which I'm used to operating. It's a psychological drama and I don't see how I, with no influence over your brother, could wield over him any more authority than you, whom he loves and of whom he is loved. I'm no hypnotist!"

"I know," Jacques Barrois protested sharply, "that you're a great psychologist."

"My God!" said Chantecoq. "It may be, indeed, that I'm blessed with a certain capacity for reasoning and even some persuasive skill. I put them at your disposal."

"Believe me, Monsieur Chantecoq, that, my father and I, would be endlessly grateful to you."

"I promise you only one thing," declared the king of detectives, "that's to do all I can to prevent the irreparable…

But I can't make you any guarantee I'll succeed…"

"You've already accomplished so many miracles!"

"Let's say I've solved some cases…"

"You're too modest."

"Not at all. In the meantime, if you really want, I'm going to ask you to give me some information, which I need before going into action."

"Monsieur Chantecoq," replied Maurice Barrois, "I'm ready, just as you asked me, at the start of this interview, to respond to any questions you ask me."

"Perfect. Let's begin. Does your brother have any religious notions?"

"Without being a sworn atheist, he doesn't practice any religion."

"Could you in a few quick words describe his character to me?"

"Gladly. He's a very clever lad, very loyal, hard-working. He has political ambitions. He wants to be someone. But he's not one of those irritating upstarts who shrink from no shame to achieve the goal they've assigned themselves.

"His success, he intends to owe only to himself, to his personal values. He's an honest man in every sense of the word and, above all, a hard worker, pushed by the urge to conserve and enhance our heritage, and to contribute to our country's wealth and improve our quality of life…"

Chantecoq, who was listening carefully to his new client, replied, "Is he in good physical health?"

"Excellent. Apart from the usual childhood illnesses, he's never been sick. Very sporty, but without excess, he's never indulged in any abuse. The old Latin maxim can be applied to him: *Mens sana in corpore sano*[2]…"

"Very well," said the king of detectives, who seemed entirely satisfied with these details. "Now, let's talk a little about your sister-in-law. You told me she's beautiful and that you believed her to be faithful."

"That's right!"

"As a consequence, until this day, nothing in her conduct, in her speech, or in her attitudes could have led you to suspect that she was unfaithful to your brother?"

"Nothing… absolutely nothing!"

"Then she must have been the very incarnation of deceit."

"Indeed… my brother told me that, the night before, she asked him to take her to the theatre and then to have supper in a fashionable cafe. My brother agreed and he told me they spent a charming evening together, a truly romantic evening!"

"Then it can only be," suggested Chantecoq sharply, "that Madame Barrois was blessed with a rare capacity for hypocrisy. So long as…"

But then he stopped suddenly.

"So long as…?" repeated his client.

But the king of detectives didn't seem disposed to venture on to ground that he had not scouted sufficiently. He replied, "Did your brother and sister-in-law have any enemies?"

"Not to my knowledge… they were well-liked, highly-esteemed… However, living largely for each other, they didn't keep up many relationships, and were seen only rarely out and about."

"And this Gomez Stardo?"

"It was just this morning that I heard his name for the

---

[2] Trans: A healthy mind in a healthy body.

first time."

"Would you be so kind, Monsieur Barrois, as to give me your address…"

"37, Rue Marillo…"

"Thank you…"

"You're not taking a note of it?"

Chantecoq replied with a smile full of finesse, "I've a memory which allows me to never write anything… not even my list of appointments."

"That's marvellous!"

"A simple gift of nature," said the bloodhound. And in a tone full of courtesy, he added, "I believe, for the moment, we don't have much else to say to each other."

Maurice Barrois stood up.

Chantecoq, doing likewise, continued. "I'm going to ask you to be so good as to return to your brother, I'll join you in around an hour…"

"Agreed…"

But, as if sudden inspiration had struck him, Chantecoq cried, "Or rather, no… I'll come with you at once. I want to be there when he wakes up. You can tell him who I am…"

The king of detectives rang stridently in the study.

The great private detective grabbed the receiver and listened. Then he said to his visitor, "They're asking for you, monsieur!"

Maurice Barrois took the receiver and listened. Chantecoq heard him murmur, "Yes, father, it's me…"

And he remained silent.

Almost at once his face expressed unspeakable dread, while these words escaped his lips, "That's awful! Horrible! My poor brother! The poor woman! Yes, I'll come back at once!"

With a trembling hand, he hung up the telephone. Then, pale, overwhelmed, he turned to Chantecoq and said in a shaky voice, "My father just told me that my sister-in-law died suddenly, an hour ago, under the arcades of Rue de Rivoli, opposite the Ministry of Finance."

The king of detectives gave a sudden start. Maurice Barrois ~~replied~~, "I'm going to return home at once. —continued Doubtless, Monsieur Chantecoq, we'll need you to shed light on this mystery. It may be that my sister-in-law killed herself... or... You see I'm so struck down by the news of this catastrophe, I'm incapable of thought. May I still count on you?"

Chantecoq replied, "Do you want me to give you my opinion?"

"I beg you..." implored the great industrialist's son.

"Very well!" declaimed the king of detectives, "if you want to avoid a scandal, *keep it quiet and don't try to find out any more!*"

Maurice Barrois looked into the face of the detective, whose eyes, clear and bright, reflected magnificent intelligence and superb loyalty. And he said,

"You're right, Monsieur Chantecoq. To protect the memory of the deceased and to preserve her name from all blemishes, such must be our duty. We'll do it."

Seriously he added, "In my father's name and in my own, I thank you sincerely for the excellent advice you just gave me. I know my father and brother well enough to confirm that it will be followed to the letter."

Maurice Barrois held out his hand to the bloodhound, who gripped it with genuine sympathy.

When Chantecoq had led the visitor to his study door, he returned to his desk, before which Météor was already standing, his notebook in hand, having sprung from heaven knows where. And the detective's secretary cried out,

"Boss, this is surely another blow struck by the Ladykiller!"

3 WHERE WE SEE CHANTECOQ DECIDE TO TAKE ON A CASE IN WHICH HE HAD PROMISED NOT TO MEDDLE

The great bloodhound folded his arms over his chest; and, while nodding, he said to his secretary,

"So! You worked that out all on your own!"

Météor riposted, "I believe, boss, that I've not demonstrated any extraordinary clairvoyance… Madame Barrois was cheating on her husband…"

Chantecoq shrugged his shoulders disdainfully. Météor thought, "I feel as though I've just made an error or said something daft."

Slowly, the greatest policeman of modern times replied, "Madame Barrois did not betray her husband."

"Eh?" Météor said, with a start.

"You seem unconvinced," Chantecoq insinuated.

"No, boss… as it was you who said it. However…"

He trailed off, fearing, by finishing his thought, that he

might provoke his employer's ill humour.

That employer prompted him, "Come on, out with it!"

"It bothers me a bit…"

"Why?"

"Because I wouldn't want, boss, for you to believe for a single moment that I'd presume to contradict you."

"Contradict me!" exclaimed the king of detectives. "Contradict me! Not only do you have the right to do so, but also the duty. How many times have I charged you to play *devil's advocate* around me, to expose me and to oppose me with all the arguments, serious or not, that pop into your head? I don't have the idiotic pretension to believe I never make mistakes. Those who pretend never to be mistaken are prideful and, as a result, imbeciles.

"For the three years you've been my student, you've given me enough proof of your intelligence, devotion, skill, audacity and initiative, for me to allow you, to ask you, and if needs be to order you to lay out objections and to contradict me. Because I no longer view you as a disciple… but as a colleague."

Overcome with gratitude, the excellent Météor was about to rush towards his master's hand, to shake it and perhaps even to kiss it.

That title of *colleague* that he had so desired to hear from he whom he had made his god and which resounded in his ears far sooner than he would ever have dared to hope, literally transported him to a joyful excess.

But Chantecoq stopped him, by saying, "Effusions can come later. Let's get to work!"

He sat at his desk. As Météor was still standing, his boss said to him, pointing out a chair directly opposite him, "Sit down there."

Météor obeyed.

"Now," said Chantecoq, "you have the floor."

"Boss," began the young secretary, "I heard the conversation you just had with Monsieur Maurice Barrois, which you charged me to take down stenographically, as I do each time a new client introduces themselves. After what he revealed, it appeared to me that his sister-in-law's guilt was clear. So I was deeply surprised when you declared that she wasn't guilty…"

"I understand. Because all appearances are against her."

"Aren't they though, boss?"

"I'll grant you that," said Chantecoq.

With a tone of the most absolute conviction, the king of detectives declared, "And yet, I'm sure that it's quite otherwise."

"That's splendid!"

"What's splendid about it?"

"Three things, boss: first, that it is; second, that you're aware of it; third, that you said nothing of it to her brother-in-law…"

Chantecoq, whose eyes glittered with mischief, riposted, "I'll answer your three points and you'll see just how right I am."

"I don't doubt it, boss. Don't I take everything you affirm as an article of faith? And even if you explain nothing to me, I'd be ready to swear on my life that the poor young woman wasn't unfaithful to her husband. You tell me, that's enough for me… So, if it tires you to talk about it…"

"Not at all," the king of detectives interrupted sharply. "I consider, rather, that you must be fully informed, for the simple reason that I have decided to pursue Madame

33

Barrois's murderer…"

"The Ladykiller?"

"Precisely, the Ladykiller."

"So much the better…"

Météor, with his usual frankness, added, "I won't pretend I was comfortable to observe your disdain for the case, which promises to be one of the most significant and perhaps the most notorious of our time. I was saddened to think that someone other than you might be called upon to unmask this monster. So, I can't tell you how happy I am that you're finally triggered!

"What a fine time we're going to have together! Or rather that I'm going to have at your side! Because you'll get him, as you got the others… like you get them all, the devil included, if you ever had the mission or inclination to go after him!"

Without appearing to pay the slightest attention to his collaborator's enthusiasm, to which, after all, he was accustomed, Chantecoq replied, "Météor, you have one great failing…"

"Tell me quickly, boss! So I can cure myself of it."

"You always have this habit, when we're discussing a subject, to stray from it…"

"Sorry, boss, I'll do everything possible to correct this dreadful habit."

Smiling benevolently, the great bloodhound continued with his customary precision. "In the meantime, let's return to the question. That of the innocent victim. I'm going to recount a sad family drama. Here it is in all its detail and entirety. Two years after his son Jacques married Mademoiselle de Beaurevoir, Monsieur Barrois the father learned from a friend, who would have done better to keep his mouth shut, that his daughter-in-law had a scoundrel brother.

"This black sheep, sent to the colonies by his parents, as much to be rid of him as to force him to earn a living, had led a fractious existence in Saigon, and in two different towns in Indochina.[3]

"He had even been compromised in a case of theft, and sentenced to five years in prison. After serving his sentence, he returned to France and, instead of rehabilitating himself by earning an honest living, he again preferred gambling and running the risks of a lifestyle more of an interloper. His father and mother were dead, so this villain only had his sister left for family...

like that.

"She, unbeknown to her husband and everybody else, undertook to save him. It's all very noble, very touching... but prodigiously unwise. Secretly, Madame Jacques Barrois came to me, and asked me to help recover the child, or rather the prodigal brother. I didn't take long to find him.

"This poisonous flower was blooming among the wildlife of the underworld, where he was pretending to be Argentinian and calling himself Gomez Stardo.

"I gathered some information on him so dreadful that I advised Madame Barrois to have nothing more to do with this brother, who appeared to me to be unsavable and wasn't hesitating, to get by, to be entertained by elderly ladies and even to despoil them, very craftily, of their jewels, every time the opportunity presented itself.

"This young woman responded that she had sworn to her parents, on their deathbed, never to abandon her brother... and that she could not fall short of such an oath. I advised

---

[3] "French Indochina" comprised Vietnam, Laos, and Cambodia. France's colonial history did not end well.

her to tell her husband everything. She refused, because she was afraid that he too would deter her from a mission that she considered sacred. I begged her to be extremely careful and I didn't hide the dangers to which she would expose herself. She didn't listen. She was wrong. You just learned the results of her obstinacy. Now, you're as informed as I am on the background to this case…"

"That's splendid," murmured Météor, very impressed by his employer's account.

While fixing him with his penetrating stare, Chantecoq continued. "From your twitching nose, or rather your flaring nostrils, I guess, oh Météor, that you still have some questions to ask me…"

"Boss, I wouldn't want to abuse…"

"Take the chance while there's still time," advised the great private detective. "Because you must know me well enough to know that, as soon as I enter into action - and that won't be long now - I won't accept from you, any more than from anyone else, the slightest interrogation."

"Then, boss, I'll fling myself into the waters."

"You can. Because, as one might say, *you can swim.*"

"Wasn't it you who taught me?"

"Get to the point, Monsieur Endless Chatter."

"Here it is, boss. How could Madame Jacques Barrois have received at her home, in her conjugal bed, the individual forbidden above all others, her own brother?"

Chantecoq replied, "He turned up at her home in her husband's absence. Madame Barrois, fearing scandal, through the goodness of her heart, would not have wanted to reject him. Having doubtless come to demand some sum of money, he obtained it. Feigning warm gratitude, he kissed her!

36

"Returning unexpectedly, Barrois must have confused this fraternal affection with the hallmarks of the most complete conjugal betrayal.

"The brother hastened to flee… The young lady, bewildered, terrified, through her panicked attitude, only accentuated her husband's conviction. And when she tried to explain herself… it was too late!

"That's how I see the matter… do you see, now?"

Météor replied, "As clearly as if I'd been there myself."

"And then, just as I was about, in a few words, to reassure Monsieur Jacques Barrois, to bring him clear, absolute proof of his wife's innocence, I learn that she has died, murdered, as you guessed, by the Ladykiller! That's why I'm declaring war on this mysterious executioner of adulterous women as, in his blindness, his rage, his dementia, he has sacrificed an innocent."[4]

"Bravo, boss!" the secretary applauded. "I recognise you again. You are and will always be the heroic and selfless champion of noble causes."

Chantecoq declared, "I can be all the more so, thanks to the fortune I've earned by recovering various necklaces and jewels, that so many vicious and dotty American women let fall into the hands of sinister one night stand lovers. However, as you already noticed, I'm never so happy, so at ease, as when I'm working for glory."

"You're not only the greatest detective of all time, you're a great, a very great artist."

---

[4] Regular readers will have surmised by now that, despite the surprising amount of agency Bernède gives some female characters, he was very much the product of his time and society. Refusing to go after a murderer because they're only killing cheating wives is, however, a new low. Sorry. It gets better.

"I'm quite simply an honest man."

"All the same," insisted Météor, "the Ladykiller must be a bit out of the ordinary! For him to succeed so quickly in discovering not that Madame Barrois had been unfaithful to her husband, but had given that appearance, and that one hour later he sent her into the next world… he must be both very 'cheeky' and very well-informed."

"That's my opinion," agreed the famous bloodhound.

Météor observed, "He must have informers who tell him about the most interesting cases."

"Error!" the king of detectives cut him off. "The Ladykiller operates alone. Just like his predecessor, the English Jack the Ripper. You see, think a little. Such a bandit can't have accomplices. He would be too fearful of being denounced."

"So, how can he act so swiftly? It's obvious he's not striking at random."

"On that last point, my lad, I'm completely in agreement with you, and that's the key to the whole mystery. I'll add that it won't be easy to find…"

"Doubtless the Ladykiller has a trick…"

"Very likely!"

"But what?"

"There we are," emphasised Chantecoq. "That's what we have to discover. I'm going to reflect on this and prepare, or at least try to prepare a plan of campaign, while you go and transpose the stenography of my conversation with Maurice Barrois… Can you do it in two hours?"

"Just about…"

"No need to rush. At the moment I'm in the position of a writer who, obliged to write a novel, finds himself before his first blank page with his pen in his hand, but with little to no inspiration within him. It's therefore a case of forcing my synapses… May the gods inspire me!"

"They'll inspire you, boss!"

This time, Météor didn't have a chance to vanish. Chantecoq, putting his hand on his shoulder, said to him, "I forgot one detail. It's likely I'll be forced to leave before you finish your task."

"What should I do, in that case?" asked the secretary.

"Wait for me and request a very good dinner for us from our good and dear cook Marie-Jeanne Gautrais. Because I imagine that, from tomorrow night, we'll be entering the fray."

"Boss," exclaimed Météor, his face joyful, "I wager you've already got something…"

"Get out of my sight… now," ordered the king of detectives.

Météor didn't need to be told twice. In three seconds, he had vanished behind the curtain. Left alone, Chantecoq, as was his habit each time he had to focus his thought on a point as important as it was defined, began to pace up and down his study.

He was so absorbed in his reflection that he didn't think to light his pipe. Once, he stopped to murmur a few words that trailed off and to which it would be impossible to supply a conclusion. Then he resumed his ambling, brows furrowed, eyes shining, burning with inner fever.

After half an hour, he went to sit at his desk, plunged his head in his hands and thought further for several minutes.

Finally, he raised his head. His brows were relaxed. His face even reflected a certain satisfaction. A slight smile flickered over his lips, and in the light of his penetrating gaze one could even make out a dash of mischief. Soon, he murmured, as though he was talking to himself,

"I've not yet found anything interesting, but there's one thing I'm sure of. The Ladykiller is a great chemist, and great chemists are not so numerous as…"

He stopped. "Flawed method," he said, "to base it on a principle of elimination. First, it wastes time; then, there's the risk of straying on to a false trail. So?"

This time, almost at once, he spoke these words which were incomprehensible for anyone other than he, "The Chain. By Jove! There's nothing but the truth in that…"

The king of detectives had certainly just discovered some happy clue. Indeed, he seemed happier. And, grabbing his telephone, he asked for a number: it was that of Monsieur Auguste Barrois.

4 WHERE CHANTECOQ
ENTERS THE FRAY

In a large office in the Imperial style, with furniture made from mahogany with leather inlays, with heavy and dark drapes, two men met: one sat at a desk whose gilded feet represented chimeras, a man of sixty years, with a beard that was grey and trimmed into the fan style worn before the war by rich agents of change, great financiers and powerful industrialists.

A deep pain was imprinted on his face and it was easy to guess that a terrible catastrophe had struck him, yet without bowing his broad shoulders and attenuating the brightness of his gaze.

This was Monsieur Auguste Barrois, father and father-in-law of Jacques and Marie-Louise.

Addressing Chantecoq, who was sitting opposite him on the other side of the table, he said, "Monsieur, I don't know how to express my gratitude for not having waited one moment to bring me the truth, however dreadful. My daughter-in-law's supposed culpability had indeed stupefied and overwhelmed me. I had, I can tell you, a foreboding there were mysterious undercurrents in that story, that my son could well have been the subject or the victim of a lamentable error.

"You demonstrated to me that I was not mistaken in reasoning thus. My endless thanks to you. Now, for me, it's not a guilty party, but an innocent for whom my son will weep.

"Certainly, that's only a feeble consolation for the atrocious sorrow which grips him; but at least it will allow him to go to the tomb of the departed to spill all the tears he needs, and to keep a pure memory of she who, unjustly slandered, was murdered in the most cowardly fashion."

Chantecoq replied. "Monsieur Barrois, in acting like this, I have done only my duty."

The industrialist said, "According to you, Marie-Louise's murderer is indeed the invisible bandit they're calling the Ladykiller?"

Chantecoq declared, "There doesn't seem to be any reason to suspect otherwise."

"It's extraordinary," replied Monsieur Barrois, "that the police have not yet succeeded in discovering his identity and putting an end to the series of his sinister exploits."

"We mustn't blame the police too much," declared the king of detectives. "This business is so complex and involves the honour of so many families, that the situation of those that this vampire has left in his wake is extremely delicate."

Monsieur Barrois cried, "And if I asked you, Monsieur Chantecoq, to apply yourself to the search for my poor daughter-in-law's murderer, how would you answer me?"

"I would answer, monsieur," retorted the famous

bloodhound without the slightest hesitation, "Yes. I would answer that I have already started the hunt for him, and on my own initiative; because I consider it's time to be rid of this villain or this madman; and if I telephoned to request a meeting, it wasn't only to bring you proof of Madame Jacques Barrois's innocence, but also to ask for information which may be useful in the course of the investigation I have just begun."

The metallurgist replied, "You can question me, Monsieur Chantecoq. I'll tell you all that I know, that's to say very little, and will be only too happy if I can be of use."

With that direct approach which characterised him, the skillful bloodhound replied. "This morning, Monsieur Maurice Barrois, your son, told me his brother received several anonymous letters claiming his wife was the mistress of a man named Gomez Stardo."

"That's correct," acknowledged Monsieur Barrois.

"Could you tell me," Chantecoq insisted, "if those letters are still in your son's hands?"

"No," replied Monsieur Barrois.

Chantecoq gave an enquiring look. Monsieur Barrois hastened to continue. "Don't worry, monsieur, the letters still exist; my son sent them to me, so I could familiarise myself with them and they're here, in my desk drawer."

"Would it be indiscreet," asked the king of detectives, "to ask you to give me one, only one, and allow me to keep it for forty-eight hours?"

"Not at all," replied the metallurgist, who opened the drawer, took out several letters and handed them to Chantecoq, saying, "Read them all and choose whichever you think is most useful."

Chantecoq took the messages and read through them.

There were five which followed each other on successive days, observing a perfidious descent.

Let's read over the great bloodhound's shoulder.

First letter:

Monsieur, I have the honour and regret to warn you that your wife is unfaithful to you.

An unknown friend.

Second letter:

Monsieur, I have the honour of informing you that your wife is betraying you with a young blackguard called Gomez Stardo.

A sincere friend.

Third letter:

I have the honour of informing you that your wife is betraying you with one Gomez Stardo and that she recently gave him five thousand francs, which he quickly frittered away gambling.

Fourth letter:

I have the honour of informing you that your wife is betraying you with one named Gomez Stardo and that she has most recently given him a sum of five thousand francs that he has quickly frittered away gambling. I'll add that Monsieur Stardo, who is an arrant knave, is threatening Madame Barrois to bring to your attention certain letters that she was unwise enough to write to him, if she fails to pay him a sum of ten thousand francs.

Someone who wishes you well.

Fifth letter:

I have the honour of informing you that your wife is betraying you with one named Gomez Stardo and that she has most recently given him a sum of five thousand francs that he has quickly frittered away gambling. I'll add that Monsieur Stardo, who is an arrant knave, is threatening Madame Barrois to bring to your attention certain letters that she was unwise enough to write to him, if she fails to pay him a sum of ten thousand francs. I should also warn you that, terrorised by these threats, your wife has made an appointment tomorrow morning at home, at half-past nine, with this unworthy individual, Madame Barrois knowing, indeed, that you must take the train to Lille around eight o'clock.

Someone who would not want your honour to be sullied.

Chantecoq, his reading finished, replied. "It's endlessly curious. When one is blessed with a few notions about graphology and examines these letters closely, it's rather easy to see that two of them, the second and the last, are not in the same handwriting.

"I'll therefore ask you, dear monsieur, so long as you don't see any inconvenience, for permission to take away this entire repugnant correspondence."

"If I understand your intent correctly," replied the master of forges, "you're going to try, thanks to those two different hands, to identify the two people who wrote them."

"Monsieur Barrois," replied Chantecoq, in an urbanely charming tone, "do remember that, when you previously asked me to recover those stolen deeds, the one condition I put on accepting that mission, was that you would not pose

45

me the slightest question during my enquiry."

"I remember," replied the metallurgist, "and please forgive me if I didn't remember sooner."

"Oh! Monsieur Barrois, I understand all too well: it is I who should beg your pardon for being so intransigent on this principle, which is one of the bases of my investigative model. Indeed, one question necessarily leads to another and, if one is so unfortunate as to slip on this slope, not only does one lose a considerable amount of time in pointless blather, but there's a serious risk of losing the thread of one's ideas and venturing on to the wrong paths."

"That's all very well-reasoned," agreed the father of Maurice and Jacques. "Take those letters, then; make of them whatever use you can and keep them for as long as may be necessary."

"I said forty-eight hours," repeated the illustrious bloodhound. "It could well be that I bring them back much sooner."

"There's no need to tell you," replied the industrialist, "how behind you I am in spirit."

"I'm sure of it, and it may be that during the course of this investigation, I will have further need to meet with you and to ask you for new information."

"I am and always shall be completely at your disposal."

Chantecoq rose, but Monsieur Barrois gestured for him to wait.

"Monsieur Chantecoq," he said, "though I promised, as you asked me, not to put any further questions to you, I'm all the same forced to ask what my attitude ought to be with regard to my son Jacques. Must I leave him believing his wife is guilty, or ought I, instead, reveal the truth?"

Chantecoq thought about it for a few seconds, then he

said, "The truth must be revealed to him; it really would be a needless cruelty to do anything other than offer him this consolation, weak as it is, and above all to let the memory of an honest woman to bear this slur any longer."

"I have a misgiving," said Monsieur Barrois.

"What's that?"

"That my son may imagine we have invented some story to diminish his pain."

"That's possible, indeed," admitted the private detective. "In that case, it would be preferable to wait until I recover this Gomez Stardo, that's to say Madame Jacques Barrois's brother. That would be physical evidence that we've spoken the truth."

"Yes, but how will you find him?" asked the metallurgist.

"That's my business," replied Chantecoq. "I can declare that it's one of my easier tasks."

Hardly had he spoken those words than there was a knock at the door.

It was Monsieur Barrois's valet, who was bringing him a letter on a platter.

The industrialist took the message and said to Chantecoq, "Will you excuse me, monsieur?"

"But of course," replied the king of detectives.

Monsieur Barrois unsealed the envelope. It contained a piece of paper folded in four, which he opened out and read:

Monsieur,

I'm the brother of Madame Jacques Barrois, of whose death I have just been notified.

I'm in a position to shed some light on this matter, details that are absolutely vital that you know.

Please accept, monsieur, my most sincere regards,

47

Viscount Albert de Beaurevoir.

Without saying a word, Monsieur Barrois passed the letter he had just read over to Chantecoq. The bloodhound examined it. The metallurgist said, "What do you make of it?"

"It's very interesting," declared Chantecoq.

"Do you believe this young man should be received?"

"Certainly."

"Good! I'm going to listen to him…"

"In that case, monsieur," said the private detective, "I'll ask your permission to be present at this interview, though without the visitor suspecting my presence."

"Nothing could be simpler," declared the father of Jacques.

And, standing, he lifted a drape which masked a door leading into a back office and study.

Then he said to Chantecoq, "You only have to sit behind this curtain and listen."

"Perfect," agreed the detective, who took a chair, went over to the drape, and settled down.

Monsieur Barrois returned to his office and said to his valet, "Show in this gentleman."

The industrialist went back to his table, wondering what the young man was going to tell him.

A few seconds later, the Viscount de Beaurevoir appeared. Monsieur Barrois stood up.

With a rather distant gesture and an attitude which was not exactly full of benevolence, the industrialist invited him to sit in the seat that Chantecoq had just vacated.

Marie-Louise's brother, who, beneath his worrying appearance of elegant delinquency, conserved a certain natural distinction that made him appear even more formidable, began, in a tone which sounded more than sincerely saddened, but profoundly sorrowful.

"Monsieur, I must thank you first for agreeing to receive me as soon as I asked. As I prepared to bring you inarguable proof that your son was the victim of a regrettable error, I learned brutally that my sister had died suddenly, in the street. I don't need to tell you how much this pains me. Marie-Louise acted with such affection towards me, such generosity and nobility. After tearing me away from the abominable existence I led and setting me back on the straight and narrow, she had just told me that she had found me a situation as honourable as it was lucrative.

"As I was kissing her with all the impetus of my gratitude and fraternal tenderness, my brother-in-law suddenly entered the boudoir where we found ourselves.

"I completely lost my head. I knew your son, like the rest of your family, was unaware of my existence. I was hidden, so ashamed were they of me, and they were right. Was I not a wretch?

"Instead of naming myself and explaining everything, I fled like a criminal, like a coward, provoking a terrible misunderstanding between my sister and your son that a single word from me would have sufficed to dispel.

"Gripped with remorse, I retraced my steps. I learned Monsieur Jacques Barrois had left home like a madman, and Marie-Louise, whose explanations he had doubtless refused to accept, had also gone out, without saying where she was going. I decided to return around lunchtime.

"No one had returned. I waited in the street until one o'clock, when a car stopped in front of your son's house. Marie-Louise was brought out, inanimate. I questioned the

49

people accompanying her. They said they had found her lying, unresponsive, under the arcades of Rue de Rivoli. They found her address in her bag she held in her clenched fingers, and brought her home at once.

"A doctor was sent for. You were alerted a few moments later, you came running. You didn't see me, I discreetly made myself scarce. I didn't enter the house. When I saw you leave with the doctor half an hour later, I guessed from your bewildered face that my poor sister had died.

"I asked around. Alas! I was not mistaken. I set about seeking out my brother-in-law. I wanted to tell him everything and above all to beg his pardon. Because it was I who, involuntarily, caused his sister's death, creating through my foolishness a situation which broke her heart.

"I couldn't find your son. So, monsieur, I have come to you."

His voice choked with sobbing, the Viscount de Beaurevoir murmured simply, "And there it is!"

Visibly moved, Monsieur Barrois replied, "Monsieur, it's not my place to condemn or absolve you, I leave to others the job of appreciating the tardy repentance that motivates you. I only wish for one thing, that the death of your unfortunate sister makes you reflect on yourself and doesn't prevent you from becoming an honest man again. Please leave me your address, because I'll ask you to repeat your declarations to my son Jacques, as soon as he's in a fit state to listen."

"I'm ready, monsieur," replied the Viscount de Beaurevoir, "and I remain entirely at your disposal. I'm living at 27 Avenue Malakoff, telephone Passy 63-86."

The industrialist noted the address and stood, indicating to his guest that the meeting was over.

The fake Gomez Stardo understood as much, because he didn't insist and, after bowing to Monsieur Barrois, who returned his salute with respect, he left the office.

The metallurgist waited to see Chantecoq come out of his hiding place; but as the curtain remained obstinately immobile, the industrialist got up and raised it.

Chantecoq had disappeared.

On the chair he had occupied during the meeting between Barrois and the Viscount de Beaurevoir, an unstamped letter-card was left, addressed to Monsieur Auguste Barrois. He tore along the dotted line and read the message which contained these simple words:

Dear Monsieur,

Forgive me for being such a poor guest; but I believed it vital to get started on an enquiry that I believe may bring useful results. A little patience, and you'll soon have news from me.

Chantecoq

Monsieur Barrois was intrigued for a moment by this missive, with its enigmatic meaning; then he began to murmur. "I believe Chantecoq may indeed discover my daughter-in-law's murderer, but, alas! That won't bring her back to life."

5 WHERE CHANTECOQ DISCOVERS THAT HIS FLAIR CAN WIN OUT OVER A DOCTOR'S DIAGNOSIS

For what reason had Chantecoq suddenly vanished into thin air?

Only he could tell us; but as we know he hates to be interrogated, we'll be careful not to pose him the question.

Let's content ourselves with following him and being passive witnesses of his actions, which, let's at least hope, will attract and retain our readers' attention.

After having left Monsieur Barrois's house, the king of detectives climbed into his Talbot 6 cylinder that he had left parked alongside the pavement and, taking the wheel, he headed to the private residence of Monsieur and Madame Jacques Barrois.

They lived in a very pleasant house, situated on Rue

Raynouard.

Chantecoq rang at the door.

A chambermaid, looking tearful, came to open the door to him.

Immediately he declared to the maid, with the imperturbable aplomb which characterised him, "I'm the police commissioner, and as Madame Barrois died on the public highway, I've come to observe the legal formalities."

The young servant, very intimidated by the title that Chantcoq had benevolently bestowed upon himself, stepped forward and said,

"Commissioner, please take the trouble to come inside. I'll take you to poor Madame."

She led him into a bedroom, situated on the first floor and where Madame Barrois lay stretched out on the bed, completely white, among the few roses that had been strewn around her in haste. On a nightstand, a crucifix between two candles, and that was all.

The chambermaid wanted to excuse herself for the lack of preparation.

"Monsieur has not yet returned home," she said. "We've done our best."

Without appearing to attach any importance to those words, Chantecoq approached the body and considered it for a while.

Soon a strange glint came into his eyes and, turning back to the maid who had not moved, he said, "Has the doctor come to examine the deceased?"

"Yes, commissioner."

"A long time ago?"

"Barely ten minutes."

"What did he say?"

"Nothing. He just signed a form."

"The burial permit."

"Yes, that's it; we're only waiting for monsieur's return in order to call out the undertaker."

"Very well," said the fake commissioner who again contemplated Marie-Louise's corpse.

Without speaking a word, he withdrew, accompanied by the chambermaid up to the door; he climbed back into his car, went back into Paris and, after having followed the docks up to the top of Pont des Saints-Pères, he turned right, crossed the bridge, went along the left bank until the top of Rue Bonaparte and stopped next to an old building from the 18th Century, whose wrought iron balconies recalled the obsolete and crumbling magnificence.

Getting out of his car, he stepped under a porte cochere; then he headed towards a stone staircase, which had kept its delicately sculpted banister and so climbed up two floors.

He stopped in front of a door on which was fixed a sign labelled: *Professor Pierre Courtil.*

He pulled a fraying bellrope. A cracked sound echoed inside; then there was a sound of slippers shuffling over the floor. The door opened slowly and revealed the classical and typical features of an old housekeeper who, a thick pair of glasses over her nose and two knitting needles jammed in her greying and rebellious hair, asked, yelling like the deaf woman she was:

"What do you want?"

Chantecoq, who immediately understood that he was dealing with someone who was 'hard of hearing', replied in a resounding clear voice, "I'd like to speak to Professor Courtil!"

The old maid, already full of regard for her visitor who,

from the outset, made himself heard so clearly, replied, "The professor is away… Oh! Not for long… He's gone to take his usual stroll along Luxembourg… But he won't be long in returning. He's as regular as a pendulum…"

Without giving Chantecoq time to breathe, the servant, who responded to the somewhat special name of Scholastic, continued in a kindly tone, "Come inside if you like. You can wait for the professor in the lounge. Unless you're too busy or you have shopping to do in the area…"

The king of detectives who, through his affable manner as much as his loud voice and perfect diction, had managed to conquer Scholastic, replied, "I have plenty of time…"

"Then do follow me…"

From the hallway, whose walls were completely hidden from floor to ceiling beneath shelves stacked with double rows of books on every subject and in every binding, Chantecoq passed into a huge room, which also formed a library, in which every book had been carefully labelled.

Doubtless it had been called a lounge because it was furnished with a large round table, with broad mahogany legs and thick, heavy marbles, and with some very worn Louis-Philippe armchairs, covered with upholstery in old-fashioned colours, the work of a modestly laborious grandmother who must have devoted numerous evenings to it and considerably advanced the point where her tired eyes demanded a pair of spectacles…

"Sit yourself down, monsieur," the servant said amiably. "Who should I say is calling?"

"Monsieur Chantecoq!" the famous bloodhound said simply.

At that name, the deaf woman gave a cry of surprise and, throwing her arms in the air, she said, "What, it's you, the

55

great detective!"

"Ah! Yes, it's me!"

"Oh! My goodness!" exclaimed Scholastique, "I'd never have suspected that you were Chantecoq. I even believed you never really existed and that all the stories the papers print about you were just blarney, invented to keep the readers happy…"

"Well then, you were mistaken, my good lady," the detective replied with a smile. "Chantecoq is no fictional character imagined by journalists in need of copy. He is well and truly alive. He is here before you, in the flesh, as they say in cinema."

As the old maid, petrified with stupefaction, stood before him, arms dangling and mouth hanging open, the king of detectives asked, "Do you think Professor Courtil will want to see me?"

"I'm sure of it," affirmed Scholastic. "He makes a principle of seeing everyone, and everyone comes here… and all sorts. You'll see, they'll fill the lounge, the dining room and the hallway. Sometimes, they queue on the landing and staircase. He's such a great scholar! If he wanted, he'd have been a rich millionaire a long time ago, but he doesn't care much for money…

"He has some small rental income which is enough to live on. He has no needs. Science, as he often puts it, is his only aim, his only love! There are those who claim he's barmy, but that's not true. He's a man unlike others, I acknowledge, but simply because he's better and wiser…

"Sit, Monsieur Chantecoq. Forgive me for leaving you; but I must restore order to the professor's office. There are books on the chairs and I wonder whether soon he'll make clients sit on them. Don't worry, you arrived first, you'll be seen first. There's no jumping the queue here!"

"I thank you, my good lady!"

"Oh! You can call me Scholastic."

And Scholastic left, turning back before exiting, to contemplate the famous Chantecoq whom she had naively assumed until that moment to be an imaginary hero created by a serial writer.

Finally she left, more troubled than if she had come face to face with a king or even a simple President of the Republic.

Instead of sitting down, as his companion had asked him, the king of detectives approached one of the shelves, overloaded with two rows of books, and began to inspect the titles which, exclusively, were those of scientific works.

Let's take the opportunity to explain as briefly as possible who this Professor Courtil was, as he has been called to play an important role in this tale.

Following brilliant studies at Paris's Medical Faculty, Pierre Courtil, the son of an honourable Parisian doctor, had been a hospital intern. His ambitions didn't end there. Soon he graduated top of the class in the teaching recruitment examination, and was named Professor of Biology at the Faculty of Nancy. There he married one of the prettiest and richest young girls in the town whom he had conquered more by his moral values and great sophistication than through his exterior advantages, which did not exceed that which we'll describe as honourably average.

His wife's considerable dowry permitted him to engage in studies towards which he felt particularly attracted, which were based on the relationship between chemistry and medicine.

Without denying the usefulness of certain therapeutic

methods, and the efficacy of certain remedies, Pierre Courtil was one of those who considered that modern medicine, despite the very real progress accomplished, was far from ridding itself completely of that empiricism which has been, for so many long centuries, and is still all too often the basis of a science, whose goal ought not to be only to treat symptoms, but further and above all, to *cure*...

His great principle was: "Only life can prolong life."

Starting from this principle, the mystery of existence no longer appeared to him to be an indecipherable enigma and, in a communication that he addressed not to the Medical Academy, but to the Science Academy, he formulated a daring proposition.

"There is no infinity!"

In his view, it was solely the insufficient development of human intelligence that made us conceive that there were no limits, no beginning, no end.

This theory provoked bitter and palpitating controversies, not just in the specialist journals, but throughout the global press.

In the space of one day, the little teacher from the Nancy Faculty had become famous.

That was hardly pleasing to the pontiffs of the medical arts, who, like all other important figures, hardly like to encourage new ideas and hardy experiments.

There was a noisy and hypocritical war waged against the innovator. Against him were used tactics so loathsome that, despite the attachment he had towards his students and the admiration he inspired in them, he handed in his notice and moved to Paris where he founded a laboratory in which he could throw himself into his research with complete independence.

He lived that way in isolation and silence for several years, carefully avoiding being spoken of and patiently awaiting his time, that's to say the time where, his efforts being crowned with success, he would be able to launch at the heads of the scientific community news of the most sensational discovery destined to upset all known facts of medical science, the prolonging of human existence not thanks to drugs of a value which was more or less happy and too often harmful, but by a new treatment, based on the same nature as human existence and on the application to man of all resources from what we call the animal, vegetable, and mineral.

This great scholar, whom most of his contemporaries tried to ridicule as a charlatan or madman, was in fact a genius in every sense of the word and, even finer, he was essentially disinterested.

Anyway, the happiness that he desired so keenly, he possessed in its entirety. He had a companion close to him, who wasn't content to remain divinely beautiful, but who was further gifted with remarkable intelligence, deep sensitivity, and apparently limitless kindness, and he could work without worrying about necessities and external demands.

He continued his route in the adorable atmosphere of perfect harmony, preoccupied with an ideal that he was convinced he would attain. Because, without being proud, he felt certain of victory and he was waiting for the hour, without gall and without impatience.

It was about to strike. He was on the point, indeed, of saying to himself, "This time, I may speak; I may divulge my secret to the whole world, without fear of error; I can hold my head up against all the envious critics, all the dishonest manoeuvres, all the nasty attacks of which I've been the victim, because I've found it... yes, I've found it!"

Then an event, as dreadful as it was unexpected, turned his life upside down. One evening, on returning home, he was told that his wife whom he had left perfectly healthy in the morning had succumbed in the evening, around five o'clock, after taking tea with a friend.

Her death was attributed to a ruptured aneurysm, provoked by a stomach ulcer that was thought to be cured. The professor's despair was immense.

For several years, he vanished. None, even his close friends, managed to discover his bolthole.

It was claimed he'd gone to shut himself away in La Trappe[5], when one day very aged, completely transformed, his face shaven, his features wizened, his eyes still illuminated by the flame of his genius, he returned to Paris and installed himself on Rue Bonaparte, in the apartment that we just visited with Chantecoq.

Then, he got back to work.

Soon, miraculous cures were being attributed to him; it was even said that, having visited the bedside of dying patients, he succeeded not only in warding off their imminent death, but in giving them a whole new lease of life. He was nicknamed the *wizard*. His colleagues, and not the least illustrious of them, began to worry about his success, which threatened to become a triumph. As they couldn't accuse him of practising medicine illegally, or prevent him from visiting the sick people who asked for him, they contented themselves with putting it about that he was a madman and putting families on their guard against this

---

[5] Probably a reference to La Trappe Abbey, in Soligny-La-Trappe, the birthplace of the Trappists.

dangerous maniac, whose miraculous cures could only be attributed to happy chance or a brisk spurt of nature.

Professor Courtil didn't deign to respond to such insinuations, as perfidious as they were untrue.

Every time his help was asked for, he granted it, but only for poor people, for those who couldn't pay and principally for people whose existence was useful for others, thus accomplishing a sort of priesthood, free of charge.

Such was the man, whose sorrow was clearly inconsolable from the expression on his face, and whose pain had made him a mysterious character, quickly haloed by a legend which was still contributing to his influence over the common people.

Why had Chantecoq gone to him? We shall find out directly.

Indeed, after a wait which lasted barely five minutes, the lounge door opened and Professor Courtil, standing on the threshold, said in a serious and resonant voice to the king of detectives,

"Do come in, monsieur, you are welcome."

With a quick glance, the bloodhound examined the scholar, whom he was seeing for the first time. He was a tall man, dressed in black, emaciated, with a well-defined mouth, eyes full of light, with a large, high forehead, topped with a coronet of greying hair whose ends were just brushing the collar of his redingote.

Chantecoq, who missed no details, noticed at once that he had extremely small hands and feet, and that his buttons were of a finesse that many women would have envied. He followed him into a room which, like the hallway and the lounge, and perhaps even more so, was filled with books, of which some lay on the ground and others were piled up on a mantlepiece, in piles so high, that one wondered how they didn't topple over.

The master indicated a seat to Chantecoq and went to sit at a small black wooden desk, which resembled a notary's.

Still in his harmoniously beautiful voice, Professor Courtil continued. "Monsieur Chantecoq, I've heard a great deal about you and I'm aware of the services you have carried out for society. I also know you're an honest man and that you greatly honour a profession which others have often rendered contemptible. I suspect you come to ask me for a favour. I'm completely disposed to grant it if possible. I admit that I held you in high esteem even before making your acquaintance. I'll add, now that I've seen you, you have grown further in my estimation."

Chantecoq, enchanted by the welcome from the man known as *wizard*, replied with deference,

"My dear master, I'm touched by your welcome. I come, indeed, to ask you for a big favour."

"Speak," invited Monsieur Courtil. "I'm listening to you with the keenest attention."

The king of detectives spoke. "You will certainly have heard talk of the misdeeds of that mysterious bandit that has been dubbed the Ladykiller?"

"Indeed," replied the scholar, "I read about all him in the papers and I frankly confess that I wouldn't have attached any great importance to it if, just now, I hadn't witnessed an extremely harrowing scene which, I don't deny, moved me greatly.

"As I do every day, I was walking under the shades of Luxembourg and I was admiring a truly delightful scene, composed of a young mother, extremely pretty, playing with a ball with two children of six and five years, brother and sister, who resembled each other closely and both had the same eyes and smile as their mother.

"One of the little ones clumsily sent his ball into a flowerbed. His mother, with the handle of her parasol, was about to send it back, when she collapsed. I was nearby; I rushed to help her. She was dead. The police arrived at once and one said, 'It's another crime from the Ladykiller.'

"Another added, 'That's the third one that we've picked up in the garden in eight days.'"

The professor added, "Monsieur Chantecoq, if you've come to ask for information regarding that business, here it is. I hasten to add that I'm incapable of providing any other information."

"Yes," agreed Chantecoq, "that's understood, my dear master, but I have, myself, a conviction that you can help me greatly in uncovering this wretch."

"How so?"

"I'm going to tell you. But beforehand, may I ask, in principle, if I can count on your help?"

"Certainly," replied the professor without the slightest hesitation. "I would be only too happy to assist you in a matter of public duty and especially if I can bring you some enlightenment. However, permit me to doubt it. I'm only a scholar."

"A very great scholar," the bloodhound pointed out.

"Please, dear Monsieur Chantecoq. What I meant to say was that I never thought for a moment to involve myself in police matters and I wonder how a man devoted purely, entirely, to science, might be useful to he who has been so rightly nicknamed the king of detectives."

"My dear master," replied the bloodhound, with a smile

full of charm, "permit me to tell you with all the respect I owe you, you are committing a small error there and, when I say a small error, it's so as not to offend you. In my humble opinion, it is indeed considerable, and I believe that modern science, to the contrary, is such a precious collaborator, such a powerful auxiliary to the police that, soon, it will no longer be able to do without it."

"I admit, indeed," replied the scholar, "that all those discoveries which, from day to day, multiply with disconcerting rapidity, are obviously of considerable aid to you in your difficult task."

"You could even say," observed Chantecoq, "that thanks to them, we can achieve victories which, a few years ago, would have eluded us unfailingly. I'm not talking only of Bertillon's marvellous invention[6], which is today one of the most important foundations of our policing system, nor of automobile technology, telegraphy, the T.S.F., etc, etc; but I want to make a brief allusion to the remarkable work, so devoted, so illuminating, brought to us by our legal doctors.

"I would simply like to stop with you on one point which is preoccupying me in a very peculiar fashion and that, alone, given your magnificent works which I've followed for some time already with great admiration, you might be able to help me to elucidate in the most complete fashion."

---

[6] Alphonse Bertillon (1853-1914), a French police officer who introduced anthropometry to law enforcement, instigating a system of taking key measurements from criminals, to identify them later. He was a key figure in the notorious Dreyfus Affair, testifying as a handwriting expert for the prosecution. He was not in fact a handwriting expert, and his flawed testimony played a significant role in history's most notorious miscarriage of justice. It's baffling why Chantecoq should speak about him in glowing terms.

"So," said Professor Courtil, "you, at least, don't view me as a wizard?"

"I consider you, to the contrary, as one of humanity's greatest thinkers, and I tell you this with no trace of flattery, because I detest toadies too much to become one myself. As I don't believe in miracles, but in wonders, I can only bow before those you have accomplished and salute the greatest and proudest underrated man in science, victim of the most ignoble cabal ever recorded in the history of medicine in France."

At those words, a crease of bitterness appeared over the scholar's lips and he said, hanging his head sadly, "No man is a prophet in his own town."

"I believe," said Chantecoq, "that now no one is a prophet anywhere. Because in France, as well as in other nations, it pleases people to exalt mediocrity to the detriment of greatness.

"You're permitted to have talent, on the condition it serves industrial, commercial, financial, political, or other vested interests. But what they never want to see stand tall, is the great man, called, as much by the value of his ideas as the energy of his character, to impose his will and to strive, to half-extinguish by the blinding light of his genius the poor candles who content themselves, because they can't do otherwise, to throw their feeble light into the darkness."

"How right you are, Monsieur Chantecoq!" cried Professor Courtil, who seemed to resist the emotion that the detective's words inspired in him.

Stiffening, to keep his expression fixed in the impassivity which he seemed to want to make his perpetual mask, he added, "Necessarily, these days, we end up becoming individualists. When one is heartless, one becomes a muzzle.

When one keeps one's sensibilities, one becomes what I am, almost a martyr?"

Chantecoq insisted, "That doesn't prevent you from being, master, one of the greatest philanthropists one could hope to greet."

"Why are you telling me that?"

"Because I know that, if you refuse some sums which are almost fortunes to care for the rich, you never hesitate to shine your light on the poor, on the unhappy who appeal to you."

The scholar sighed. "Ah! If I could only care for them all, save them all!"

"You've obtained marvellous results. It's even said that you've resuscitated the dead."

At those words, Professor Courtil gave a half-smile, in which there was both great scepticism and much kindness.

"No, Monsieur Chantecoq, those who told you that, I won't say they lied to you, because it's highly likely that they spoke in good faith. I'll affirm only that they were mistaken.

"I've sometimes restored to life some people that were believed to be dead, but who were only plunged into a lethargic or cataleptic state. In this way I have avoided, despite this system of precipitous burials, which is the rule in France and elsewhere, the live burial of some unfortunates that, with good faith, were believed forever lost to us. And I'm very proud of that."

"How well I understand!" cried Chantecoq. "And I came today precisely to ask you to revive a woman whose family believes her dead, and whose death the state examiner has confirmed.

"This lady is rich. But, be assured, she deserves your interest as much as or more than any indigent. Indeed, she is

66

a victim of the Ladykiller. Now, you might not know, my dear master, that until now this mysterious bandit has attacked women who were unfaithful to their husbands."

"Now that's strange!" observed the scholar.

"An investigation I have begun has established this for me. Now, this lady, of whom I'm speaking to you, is entirely innocent; I also have proof of that and I can furnish you with it at once."

"There's no need, Monsieur Chantecoq, I'll take you at your word."

"I'm touched by your confidence and I beg you, if, before giving me your answer, you consider it necessary that I bring you all possible information on the subject of that young woman, I'm ready to give it to you."

"I repeat, there's no need. But are you really sure this woman is indeed alive?"

"Absolutely sure, no, but I have a hunch she is. I can't explain how I arrived at this conclusion. You don't yet know me well enough, Professor, but, without wanting to pass myself off in your eyes as stronger than I am, allow me to assure you, and all those who have had dealings with me will confirm it, that I'm gifted with a flair, that I won't dare qualify as infallible, but which has led me many times, without the support of any other element, on the path to the truth.

"Well! My dear master, my flair tells me that this woman is not dead. My flair tells me that the Ladykiller mistook his dose, or the nature of the poison that he made this unfortunate person swallow or which he injected into them. And I just ask you to please come to her with me, to assure yourself, if it is possible to restore her to the love of a husband whom she loves tenderly and who, by now, must know that his companion has never ceased to be faithful to him."

Before responding to the great bloodhound's highly eloquent and persuasive adjuration, Professor Courtil reflected for a few moments.

Chantecoq was waiting for his decision impatiently.

Never yet, perhaps even when he was pursuing the famous *Belphégor* through the halls of the Louvre; when he was trying to penetrate the *Mystery of the Blue Train*; when he was unravelling the enigma of *The Haunted House*, when he established the innocence of a young aviator unjustly accused of an abominable crime; when he managed to arrest so formidable a character as *Zapata* and when he put an end to the series of sinister exploits of *The Amorous Ogre*, etc, etc, yes, perhaps never yet had he been more anxious to achieve his goal.

Fearing the caprice of this man who could be only somewhat embittered by all the injustices to which he had been subjected on the part of his colleagues and the quarantine that had been imposed on his genius, Chantecoq was ruminating, in his brain, fresh arguments he could use in case his new friend failed him, when he replied in his serious and naturally sorrowful voice,

"The name of this young lady?"

"Madame Marie-Louise Barrois."

"Her age?"

"Twenty-three years."

"Brunette or blonde?"

"Blonde."

"Her height?"

"I could only give you an approximation, because I only saw her on her deathbed. She seemed rather tall to me."

"Not less than one metre seventy?"

"That's it."

"No children?"

"No."

"Can you furnish me with any information, even approximate, on her health?"

"Her father-in-law told me that it had always been excellent."

"Good."

Professor Courtil fell into thoughtful silence again, which the detective was careful not to disturb.

After a while, the scholar called out in a loud voice, "Scholastic… Scholastic…"

A door opened. The servant appeared. The professor asked her, "Are there many people waiting for me?"

Scholastic replied, "Twenty. It's as though they've all got the idea to return at once. And then, you know, that's not the end; soon, I'm sure there will be more than forty, and I'll again be obliged to make them wait on the stairs, though the concierge complains about that…"

With a decisive gesture, the scholar interrupted this flood of oratory which was beginning to escape the servant's mouth and, in a tone of voice which brooked no reply, he said,

"Tell those people they should come back this evening at five o'clock. For the moment, it's impossible for me to see them! Give them numbers, to avoid any jostling or queue-jumping."

"But, Professor," Scholastic objected, "they'll be furious. They could cut me to ribbons."

"Oh! I'm not worried. They won't say anything to you,

and I know you're more than capable of dealing with the likes of them."

With a note of peremptory authority, he intoned, "Go, do as I've told you, and let there be no more questions."

The maid went to carry out her orders.

When she had left the room, Chantecoq said simply, "So, master, you accept?"

"Yes, I accept," replied Professor Courtil.

"Thank you, from the bottom of my heart."

"Dear Monsieur Chantecoq, you'll be able to express your gratitude when the experiment has succeeded, because I make no promises."

"Very well! As for me," cried the detective full of optimism, "I'm sure of your success…"

"On the condition that this young woman is still alive…"

"She is," affirmed the bloodhound with a note of conviction which appeared to make a serious impression on his companion; because he, standing up, replied,

"Please wait five minutes and I'll be with you."

The scholar left through a small door, leaving behind the private detective, who seemed to be delighted with the results of his mission.

He said to himself, "If I'm not mistaken, what joy for me, not only to save this unfortunate, but to return her to her husband along with evidence of her innocence! Ah! These really are the best moments of our profession, those where we can do so much good!"

Five minutes later, as he had promised, the scholar returned. He was holding in one hand a felt hat with a wide brim and he called again in a loud voice, "Scholastic… Scholastic!"

The maid reappeared at once, red-faced and out of

breath. "They've left," she announced to her master, "but as I predicted, that wasn't all. The things I needed to tell them! They all said they would return this evening. I hope, professor, you'll be there to receive them. Otherwise, they're more than capable of strangling me and cutting me into pieces!"

"Scholastic," replied the scholar with the impassive serenity of an Anatole France character[7], "don't get in such a state; I promised to be there at five o'clock this evening, I'll be there! Until then, restore your calm and think about preparing a simple but hopefully succulent dinner."

"I hope Monsieur will be happy with it," said the servant.

"And now," replied Professor Courtil, addressing Chantecoq, "I'm entirely at your disposal."

They left the office, crossed the lounge and the hallway, crossed the threshold and went down the old staircase.

Once in the street, Chantecoq, opening the doors of his Talbot, said to his companion, "Climb aboard, my dear master."

"You don't have a chauffeur, then?" asked the scholar.

"No. I prefer to drive myself."

"In Paris? That must be very absorbing."

"Indeed it is," replied the king of detectives. "While I'm concentrating on not running over any pedestrians and defending myself from all manner of tiresome incidents, I don't think about anything else, and that gives my brain a rest

---

[7] Anatole France (1844-1924). Novelist, and winner of the 1921 Nobel Prize for Literature. France was popular in his time, but as a socialist he was attacked by the far-right after his death. Is Bernède (whose own politics are ambiguous but certainly right of centre) striking a moderate note with this reference?

from all the ideas thrown up by the functions that I carry out. It is, to some extent, a derivative!"

While speaking, the great bloodhound had taken the wheel and, observing that Professor Courtil was comfortably installed on the rear cushions of the car's interior, he started his motor and soon reached the home of Monsieur and Madame Jacques Barrois.

In the hallway, they crossed paths with the great industrialist who, noticing Chantecoq, went over to him, holding out his hand, and saying, "I couldn't help telling my son that his wife was not to blame. He just had a definitive explanation from his brother-in-law. At the moment he is praying at the funereal bed and I believe it would be better to leave him alone and not interrupt his tears, which are comforting him morally and physically, and transforming his dreadful despair into a sorrow that softens the thought that he has no reproach for she who has left him forever."

"Monsieur Barrois," replied Chantecoq, "you're aware that I've decided to uncover your daughter-in-law's murderer."

"I know, and I can only encourage you on this path."

While pointing out Professor Courtil to Monsieur Barrois, who was standing a little distance away, the bloodhound continued. "With this aim, and for another reason, that I can't yet divulge, I need you to allow me a few moments alone with my friend and collaborator that you see here in the funerary bedroom of your daughter-in-law... If it's not an abuse of your accommodating nature, I would ask you to stay away."

"For how long?"

The scholar interjected, "Around ten minutes."

Monsieur Barrois replied, "I'm going to do my best to

satisfy your request."

And, addressing a valet, he said, "Show these gentlemen into the lounge."

While the servant was carrying out that instruction, the industrialist entered the bedroom, which had been transformed into a proper chapel and in the middle of which, on a bed, Marie-Louise was lying among the flowers.

The light of numerous candles were reflecting on her beautiful face.

On hearing and recognising his father, Jacques stood and said, "Look at her, father, how beautiful she is! You wouldn't think she was dead; it's rather as though she's asleep."

He added, grabbing Monsieur Barrois by the arms, "I just told her how much I'm suffering for suspecting her, mistrusting her... Father, do you believe her soul heard me? Do you believe she will have granted me forgiveness?"

"But yes of course, my dear child," replied Monsieur Barrois. "Come on, calm down, don't stay there. Maurice just arrived, he is here; he would like to see you, to speak to you about certain decisions we can't take without you; then you can come back to your poor wife."

Gently, the industrialist led his son towards the door.

Jacques, in a broken voice, observed to him, "She'll be all on her own."

"No, I'll watch over her. Maurice is downstairs in the study; go and meet him, go... go, my child."

Jacques obeyed and left at a trailing pace, leaning on the banister, broken by the immense grief that was torturing him.

His father let him go. When he was sure that Jacques had rejoined his brother, he went down the stairs in his turn, headed to the lounge and said to Chantecoq, "Now, come with me."

73

Chantecoq and Professor Courtil followed him closely.

Moments later, it was their turn to enter the bedroom. Discreetly, the great metallurgist left them with the deceased and remained in the corridor, awaiting the result of this mysterious mission.

Professor Courtil approached the body and, taking a little pouch from his pocket, he took out a mirrored tile which he put beneath the nostrils and mouth of Marie-Louise.

No breath misted it. He showed no outward sign of discouragement or enthusiasm, but, taking from his pouch a flask which seemed to be full of water, he poured a few drops on the glass which he then wiped with a piece of cotton.

Again, he brought the mirror to the dead woman's face. To the great satisfaction of Chantecoq, who was following this experiment with palpitating interest, a veil, at first extremely light, then sufficiently opaque, spread across the mirror, which, after a few seconds, was covered with a proper fog. Then, simply, in a low voice, the professor said, "You were right, Monsieur Chantecoq, this young woman is alive."

6 MARIE-LOUISE

Chantecoq repressed a cry of joy. In a low voice, he asked the professor, "Can you restore her to life?"

"I'm sure, it will be the easiest thing in the world. In a few minutes, this young lady will have returned to her senses completely."

"That's marvellous," said Chantecoq, who, still, wasn't given to displays of ecstasy.

With great self-control, Professor Courtil declared, "This young woman, when she awakes, must not open her eyes to this funeral scene. We must carry her to another room, next to this one. Please, Monsieur Chantecoq, would you open that door and tell me where it leads?"

Chantecoq obeyed at once and, opening the door, he noticed there was a small boudoir through there, very elegant, with a divan on which it was very easy to lay out the fake corpse.

He made his discovery known to the scholar, who,

without hesitating for a moment, picked up the young woman in his arms and went to lay her down on the divan, taking care to keep her head high and her kidneys leaning solidly on cushions.

Then he took from his pouch a peculiarly-shaped syringe which contained no liquid, and was equipped with no needle and ended in a sort of metallic bulge in the shape of a suction cup that he applied to Marie-Louise's right wrist. Slowly, still silently, he pushed the plunger.

When it had been pushed to its full extent, the scholar raised the syringe of which the end had left a faint red circle on Madame Barrois's skin.

Turning to Chantecoq who, mute, immobile, had witnessed this apparently insignificant operation, he explained.

"This syringe contains a gas of my own invention, which is spreading through this young person's system and which has an effect on the circulation as direct and efficient as it is harmless. I've taken twenty years to develop it."

"Then," observed the king of detectives in a hoarse voice, "without you, this unfortunate woman was going to be buried alive?"

"Certainly."

"But that's awful."

Professor Courtil didn't reply. He fixed his ardent gaze on Marie-Louise's face, awaiting the first symptoms of a return to life.

Chantecoq continued. "Once she was in her coffin, would she have regained consciousness?"

The scholar gave a simple affirmative nod.

"What horror!" the great bloodhound couldn't help exclaiming.

And he added, "So, have all the Ladykiller's victims suffered this atrocious ordeal?"

The professor made a gesture which meant, "Silence!"

Chantecoq fell quiet and drew nearer.

Marie-Louise's face was already less livid. Just as Courtil had predicted, the circulation of the blood was beginning to resume. Her heart had resumed beating. Her limbs had already lost their corpse-like rigidity. Her nostrils were twitching almost imperceptibly, her lips, a very slight movement. Her fingers, first, were relaxing.

Swiftly the professor lifted the rosary entwined around them and slipped it in his pocket. At intervals, a few sighs raised the young woman's chest.

The miracle continued, gradually, immutably. It wasn't a corpse that the great biologist was resuscitating, but a sleeper that he was rousing from lethargy.

He turned to Chantecoq, who was petrified with admiration, and said to him, "Now you can relax completely: in ten minutes Madame Jacques Barrois will be as healthy as she was before the accident: you may warn the family."

Chantecoq left the bedroom, exuberant with joy.

He found Monsieur Barrois the father, who was continuing to keep watch in the corridor.

"Monsieur," he said, "promise me to keep calm… very calm… very in control of yourself!"

Shocked, Monsieur Barrois asked, "Why are you asking me that?"

The private policeman replied, "Because often great joys are as hard to bear as great sorrows."

"Monsieur Chantecoq, I believe I understand you, but…"

"I'm going to explain," declared the detective. "If I announced to your son and you, as well as your entire family,

77

that you lived through, not a terrible reality, but a frightful nightmare; that not only did Madame your daughter-in-law commit no fault, but that she is still alive!"

"Monsieur Chantecoq," murmured the industrialist in a stifled voice, "you're giving me vertigo... Marie-Louise would be..."

"Come with me," said the bloodhound simply, and dragged Monsieur Barrois into the bedroom at once.

Noticing that his daughter-in-law's body had vanished, the industrialist cried out, "Where is she? What have you done with her?"

Chantecoq pointed to the boudoir door which was still open. The metallurgist rushed into the room. Marie-Louise was beginning to open her eyes.

Monsieur Barrois stopped, struck dumb with shock. Chantecoq, pointing out the scholar who, his watch in his hand, was taking the young woman's pulse, cried, "This is Professor Courtil, thanks to whom your daughter-in-law is going to be restored to the bosom of her family..."

"Monsieur," replied the industrialist, approaching the doctor, "I can't believe my eyes or my ears. What, that poor child who just now I left laid out, rigid and frozen on her funeral bed, here she is... restored to life... and almost to reality!"

Hardly had Monsieur Barrois pronounced those words than Marie-Louise, parting her lips, which were gradually recovering their colour, murmured in a faint but distinct voice,

"Jacques! Jacques!"

"Monsieur Barrois, go and warn your son," Chantecoq suggested.

The industrialist left at once. Marie-Louise, who was

recovering more and more awareness of her surroundings, was again asking for her husband. She still didn't remember any recent events. Alone, her heart's instinct was inspiring her thought.

"Jacques," she repeated, "why aren't you there?"

And, while passing her hand over her forehead, she added, "My God! What happened?"

Then she glanced between the professor and the detective, who she was seeing for the first time. And yet, she was at home, in her boudoir. So, who were these strange people?

"Who are you?" she murmured in a distant voice.

Chantecoq replied swiftly, "Doctors!"

"And my husband?" she asked, fearfully.

"He's on his way," replied the bloodhound.

A cry tore from the young woman's chest. She'd suddenly just remembered the morning's terrible misunderstanding.

"He's left, hasn't he? Yes, he left… and you don't want to tell me. And my father-in-law… and Maurice. They've all abandoned me. Because they think I'm to blame!"

"No," the king of detectives said with force, "they believe you and they know you to be innocent!"

"Who are you then to speak to me like that?"

Chantecoq didn't have time to answer. Marie-Louise called out, distraught, "Jacques! Jacques!"

The industrialist's son had just entered the boudoir and rushed towards his wife, who opened her arms wide to him.

Discreetly, Chantecoq and Professor Courtil, whom Jacques hadn't noticed in his emotional state, withdrew to the next room, where Monsieur Barrois and his son Maurice were waiting.

Monsieur Barrois was the first to speak. "So, all is well?"

"Admirably so," replied Chantecoq.

"Never," the metallurgist cried, "Can we express our gratitude to you."

"It's above all Professor Courtil that you must thank," declared the king of detectives modestly, pointing at the scholar, who now seemed to have only one wish: that of disappearing, to escape the praises that were threatening him.

Chantecoq held him back, by saying, "I can't attribute to myself the success in which I played only a tiny part: because though I hoped Madame Marie-Louise Barrois was still alive, it's certain that, without you, dear master, I would have been incapable of restoring her to life."

Courtil replied coldly. "I've simply done my duty."

And after nodding to Auguste and Maurice Barrois, he said to Chantecoq, "Dear monsieur, I'm going to request the favour of driving me back home; because not for the whole world would I want to keep waiting those who need me and whom I put off until later in order to come here."

Chantecoq replied, "Of course, I'll take you back."

And addressing Monsieur Barrois the father, he added, "If you allow me, I'll return here at once, because I have quite a few things to tell you."

Monsieur Barrois and his son agreed immediately and held out their hands to the private detective, who clasped them cordially.

Professor Courtil had reached the corridor already. Monsieur Barrois murmured in Chantecoq's ear, "Who is that strange doctor you brought to us?"

"I'll explain soon," replied the bloodhound, rushing to rejoin his companion and to get back into his Talbot.

Chantecoq said to the professor, "Would you mind sitting next to me? I need to talk to you."

"Certainly, with pleasure," replied the scholar, who sat down at the detective's side.

He started his motor and, while setting off towards Rue Bonaparte, Chantecoq said to his neighbour, "I know that you don't like compliments. So I won't offer you any. However, I can't prevent myself from telling you that in the course of my long career, never yet have I been involved in such extraordinary events. If you had only been understood, my dear master, what services could you have offered to humanity! Perhaps one day you would consent to divulge and propagate your discovery?"

"I shall see," replied the professor laconically.

Chantecoq continued. "When I think that all those unfortunates plunged into lethargy by this Ladykiller, were buried, and, as you told me just now, awoke in their tomb! Though I am toughened against all physical emotions, and almost all mental shocks, I can't help shuddering.

"Because, while admitting these women were hardly innocent, don't you think the punishment that was inflicted on them by this extraordinary vigilante is truly disproportionate to their offence?"

"I have no opinion on that matter," replied the scholar.

"What a peculiar fellow," thought the bloodhound. "It's said that genius and madness are very close to each other. It's certain that at this moment, I feel as though I find myself in the presence of a man who is gifted with one and afflicted with the other."

Aloud, he said, "Under some impassive appearances, my dear master, I'm certain you're blessed with an excellent heart."

"Me?"

"Yes, you! Didn't you just prove it, by coming running so

81

quickly to tend to this young lady? I know, in any case, the benefits you spread in a world where happiness is hardly common. So wouldn't you have pity on all those poor women who strayed for one moment, who are so ferociously, so pitilessly struck down by an invisible enemy? You alone can stop his exploits."

Professor Courtil replied. "I've thought about it many times and, if I haven't done it sooner, it's because I thought my intervention wouldn't stop the criminal, and if I was busying myself with restoring his victims to life, he would change his method and, instead of plunging those women into lethargy, he would kill them straight away."

"That would already be a result," observed Chantecoq, "as it would prevent those dreadful agonies at the bottom of a coffin."

"That's very true," replied the scholar. "I hadn't thought about that, because I was convinced like everyone that this mysterious maniac killed at once; but as it is not the case, I consent, with purely humanitarian goals, to tend to the first of those unfortunates who succumbs."

Chantecoq clarified. "So you're authorising me to find the husband and offer him your support?"

"Yes," admitted the professor, "but on one condition: that this mission, as well as my intervention, remains strictly confidential. I hate publicity and I live in obscurity sheltered from scandal mongering, calumnies, that I no longer have the strength to bear.

"I've made myself an extremely calm interior and exterior life and, as the Ancient Romans used to say: I hope to live far from the tribulations of the Forum or, if you like, the public sphere."

Chantecoq replied. "Your will shall be respected, I

undertake an absolute commitment as to that. It only remains, my dear master, to take your leave and to thank you for intervening, while there was still time, in the case of this young lady, who was truly worthy of your compassion."

With a peculiar expression, Professor Courtil replied, "Monsieur Chantecoq, you're not going to take offence at what I'm about to say to you?"

"I have an excellent character."

"Very well! You appear to me as an ever more astonishing man."

"How so?"

"I'll tell you. You've given at least twenty-five years of service to police work, both private and for the state."

"Exactly twenty-seven," declared the king of detectives.

"And you've retained such generosity?"

"Why not?"

"It's strange!"

"And many of my colleagues, dear master, I would say even the majority, are very brave people who know, when they must, to take pity on those who deserve it."

Monsieur Courtil continued. "I would have thought, to the contrary, that by rubbing shoulders with criminals, one would end up, not becoming a criminal oneself, but at least by losing almost entirely and even completely all sensitivity."

"My dear master," cried Chantecoq, "there you committed, allow me to tell you, not just an error, but further an injustice."

"I can see that."

"We don't only have dealings with scoundrels; we also deal with many honest people and we realise they form the overwhelming majority. Unfortunately, not having that lack of scruples which characterises the relentless bandits after them, they generally don't know how to defend themselves, any more than a flock of sheep knows how to ward off a wolf's attack.

"It's precisely that sort of ingenuity that characterises the good ones and causes their inferiority in the face of evil. That makes detectives, private or not, accessible to those feelings of humanity which you were so surprised to perceive in me."

Professor Courtil cried out, "Now, Monsieur Chantecoq, I understand you completely, and I congratulate myself on having provoked your explanations. I'll confess to you I was feeling, as do certain people who are unaware, an instinctive apathy for everything connected to the police; I recognise that you have, in a few moments, transformed it into a deep and sincere sympathy, which demands only to be extended over all those who constitute the guardians of social order."

"On that happy note," declared the great bloodhound, "I'll ask permission to take leave of you; because I have several errands to run which won't allow further delay. Forgive me for having held you up for so long; that conversation was vital. Now, we can march onward hand in hand; because I've not forgotten your promise. Perhaps, thanks to you, I can achieve the goal I've assigned myself, to disrupt the Ladykiller's operations and perhaps also unmask him."

Monsieur Courtil nodded in agreement; then, getting up, he held out his hand to Chantecoq, who shook it effusively.

Professor Courtil, after watching the detective vanish into the distance, murmured to himself, "Decidedly, this man is one of the most intelligent and most honest I've ever met. But I doubt he'll ever get his hands on the Ladykiller."

7 WHERE CHANTECOQ PROCEEDS WITH A PROBING INVESTIGATION WHICH BRINGS A RESULT HE WAS HARDLY EXPECTING

On leaving Professor Courtil, Chantecoq returned directly to the home of Monsieur and Madame Jacques Barrois, where he was welcomed with enthusiasm by the young couple, who owed him the complete restoration of their happiness, as well as by Monsieur Auguste and Maurice Barrois who didn't know how to express their gratitude to him.

At once, Chantecoq told them, "Know that I'm very happy with the result, however, I've not come here to celebrate or to receive your congratulations, however precious they are to me, but first and foremost to *work*."

Monsieur Barrois the father asked, "Be convinced, Monsieur Chantecoq, that we'll do everything to facilitate the task that you've assigned yourself, that is to say, the Ladykiller's arrest.

Jacques Barrois added, with his wife's approval, "It's the

best way to express our gratitude."

The king of detectives replied. "You authorise me to pose certain questions, Madame Barrois?"

"Gladly," agreed Jacques.

"And," declared Marie-Louise, "I consider it my duty, monsieur, to answer as best I can."

"Then all is well," cried the great bloodhound with a joyous air. "I can begin my examination?"

"At once," said the young wife with a smile.

Chantecoq began. "Without wanting to relive events whose memory must be painful, I would be very happy, madame, if you could give me the exact itinerary you followed, when you left home this morning."

"I'll try to recall it," Marie-Louise responded, "I confess I was so troubled at that time! It could be therefore that there are a few holes in my memory. The truth is that on leaving my house so suddenly, I had only one desire: to find my husband and tell him everything.

"Unfortunately, I was so overwhelmed that I didn't think for a single instant of going to the places where I had the best chance of finding him, that's to say at his father's or his brother's home.

"I took a taxi and I went to his office, on Rue de Castiglione. There I was told he had not yet arrived. In spite of that, I went into his office, which was empty. A voluminous pile of mail was waiting for him, proving that I had been informed accurately.

"I waited for a while. Still no one! When the office junior came to inform me, with an embarrassed tone, that Monsieur Jacques had been taken ill at his brother's house, and that he would not be coming that morning, I was completely panic-stricken. Then, I took Rue de Rivoli, walking at a nervous pace under the arcades, when at some point, I felt myself gently jostled by an old gentleman with a white beard who apologised and went on his way, without me lending the slightest attention to the incident.

"I took a few steps, and I was about to hail a cab to take me to my brother-in-law, when I felt the ground vanish from beneath my feet, and I crashed to the ground like a lead weight. That's all I can tell you, Monsieur Chantecoq."

The detective replied, "Thank you, madame, for the good grace with which you answered me. I'll ask nothing more of you today, and I'll let you savour in peace your happy life that is restored."

He stood, deferentially kissed the hand that Marie-Louise offered him, clasped those of the three men and withdrew, looking satisfied although at first glance he had gathered only some very vague information, which hardly seemed of a nature to put him on the trail of the criminal he had tasked himself with tracking down. He returned home at dinner time. Chantecoq had one principle: when he was at table, except on very rare exceptions, he never spoke of the cases with which he was dealing.

Météor, who was sharing his meal, knew him far too well to frame the slightest question; but he couldn't help noticing that his boss, as he called him, was in excellent spirits and was doing justice, with the appetite of a twenty-five year old, to the succulent menu that had been prepared for him by Marie-Jeanne, a qualified cordon bleu cook, and the happy wife of Pierre Gautrais.

After dinner, Chantecoq, while lighting his pipe, said to Météor, "Now, my lad, let's go through to my study. We have work to do."

Both of them went into the room that we described

earlier.

Chantecoq sat down and at once asked his secretary, "Did you finish writing up your stenography?"

"Yes, boss, it's right there in front of you, in that blue folder."

"Perfect!"

Chantecoq dove into reading this document; Météor, who had lit a cigar, maintained a religious silence. When Chantecoq had finished, his pipe had gone out. He refilled it with care, lit it with precision and, after taking a few puffs which went drifting into the air, he said,

"This case, which seems so shadowy, is, to the contrary, of an infantile simplicity."

Météor couldn't hold back a gasp of astonishment.

"That surprises you?" said Chantecoq, casting an eye glinting with mischief at his student.

"Whatever you say, boss, I don't have your perspicacity, or your flair…"

"It's not a case of flair in this circumstance," corrected the king of detectives, "but of reasoning, of pure logic. In any case, it's very excusable that you didn't grasp it at once, as you are in complete ignorance of the investigation that I carried out this afternoon, as well as some events which have come about as a consequence.

"As you have not really been called on to play an active role in this case thus far, I'm therefore going to bring you up to date with what happened, and I will give you the opportunity to draw a conclusion from it all which, I'm sure, will conform with my own."

"Boss, it goes without saying that I've never listened to you with such complete attention."

Chantecoq related to his collaborator the first visit he

made to the private home of Monsieur and Madame Jacques Barrois, the intuition he had that Marie-Louise was not dead, the approach he had made with success to Professor Courtil, Marie-Louise's resurrection, and, finally, the details she had given him.

When he had finished, he said to Météor, "Now, you have the floor."

The student detective appeared rather embarrassed.

"Boss," he said, "forgive me; you're going to think and perhaps tell me once more that I'm only a ninny, but, there's nothing for it, I'm obliged to talk frankly. Indeed, if I declared to you that I also found this case quite simple, you wouldn't hesitate to ask me why. And I would be embarrassed to respond to you, because, contrary to you, I don't see anything clear about it, not at all... I understand only one thing: that you were lucky to meet on your travels a kind of wizard, who revives people plunged into lethargy. One point, that's all.

"There's also that tale of the old gentleman who jostled Madame Barrois under the arcades of Rue Rivoli and I believe for my part that this must have been the Ladykiller and that all the hair he was wearing on his chin were those that we call... mobile hair. But all that doesn't tell me who he is, and if I had only some similar clues, I would be hard pressed to know where to direct my research."

"Météor, Météor," said the famous bloodhound with a sigh, "although you've made immense progress, especially in the last year, and you've become an auxiliary that I would call my right hand, I perceive that you still have a great deal to learn."

"Boss, that's exactly what I think."

"Very well! My boy, for this evening, we'll go no further. I want, indeed, to give you a lesson in police experience, which will certainly help much more than if I presented you with all my ideas.

"Practice, you see, is the only way to improve. I'm persuaded that, when you've seen me manoeuver, you'll know much more than if I had signalled my intentions to you in advance."

"So," exclaimed the young secretary in a disappointed tone, "while you're going to work, I'm going to be obliged to cross my arms?"

"I didn't say that, quite the opposite. From tomorrow morning, you're going to be in the field and I'm about to explain, right now, what you'll have to do."

"Boss, I'm happy."

"Oh! It's not the first class task."

"Too bad."

"But it's no less important. This Professor Courtil, of whom I spoke to you just now, after having obtained brilliant success, I will even say too brilliant success, was forced, in response to a coalition of jealous colleagues, to take a sabbatical of several years. I would like to know... first: if he has told the complete truth about the motives behind his retirement. Second: Where he went to live, and what he was doing during those twelve years in seclusion."

"Understood, boss," replied the secretary.

And arming himself with his notebook and a pencil, he added, "I'll ask you only to be so kind as to give me the address of the person in question."

Chantecoq nodded. "37 Rue Bonaparte. I'll warn you that he has as a servant a certain Scholastic, who appears to be very devoted to him, and who must obviously be aware of all the mysteries in his life. It's through her, I'm convinced, that you'll inform yourself."

"Boss, there's a lead for which I must thank you, because it simplifies my task greatly."

"Now," concluded Chantecoq, "although it's still early, let's go to bed and let's make a serious provision for sleep, because there would be nothing astonishing if we end up needing to endure several all-nighters."

"So, good evening, boss!"

"Good evening, my friend."

They were about to separate, Chantecoq to reach his bedroom which was situated on the first floor, and Météor to go to his own which was on the second, when, in spite of himself, Météor exclaimed,

"Oh, it's certain, I'm just an idiot."

"Why do you say that?" asked the king of detectives with a smile full of affectionate indulgence.

"Boss, all of a sudden, as they say in the old melodramas, a little light came on inside my head."

"What light?"

"Very well! Boss, I acknowledge like you that this case is one of blinding clarity."

"Well, well," said the fine bloodhound in an ironic tone.

"And if I dared," continued Météor, "I'd tell you that if you have spotted the Ladykiller, well! I too have done the same, and it's…"

He stopped, as though he didn't dare speak aloud the name of the incriminated person. Chantecoq burst out laughing, and replied, "It's you!"

"Oh! Boss, you're joking!"

"Of course I'm joking, and if I'm joking like that, it's to prevent you from saying something daft. You're convinced, aren't you, that Professor Courtil is the Ladykiller?"

"Damn, boss, as you're asking me to investigate him, I conclude that, at the very least, you suspect him; and when you suspect someone, it's much the same as accusing them."

"Météor, my boy," declared Chantecoq with a severity which was barely apparent, "let me give you a piece of advice! Beware imagination. It's a faculty which can grant immense services to those who possess it, but it can also cause the most tiresome problems.

"Remember this: when one is leading an investigation, one must not have a preconceived opinion in advance; you need a *tabula rasa* free from all ideas, to envisage only reality and to embark on the deductions boat only when one is sure of one's foundations.

"If you set off tomorrow with this principle that Professor Courtil is the Ladykiller, you will necessarily end up making an inquiry that is incomplete, fragile, unsubstantiated, because you will have anticipated its results in advance.

"Therefore I forbid you, do you hear me, from accusing this man, against whom, in any case, I have no kind of proof, nor even a presumption, which permits me to bring on him such a decisive and terrible judgement.

"As I'm called to have some interesting dealings with him shortly, I want, not exactly to learn what makes him tick - I know that - but I would like to be informed about him, in such a way that nothing from his past is unknown to me; one point, that's all… you understand me?"

"Yes boss, and as always, you're wisdom itself. Thanks to you, I'm already embarked, because if you hadn't spoken as you just did, I believe I would have made a complete mess of it."

"On that note, I'll wish you a good night."

"And to you too, boss."

Chantecoq, instead of going up to his room, as he had first intended, lingered in his study; then, after reflecting for a few moments, he muttered,

"I definitely believe that little Météor will go far… if he listens to me!"

***

Earlier, while Chantecoq was preparing to eat a well-earned meal, a drama, as strange as it was terrible, was unfolding in a great dance hall on the Champs-Elysées.

A young lady, belonging to the highest aristocracy, Baroness Véra d'Ormoix, was in the middle of executing a fox-trot with one of the establishment's staff dancers, when, suddenly, she collapsed to the ground.

People hurried over, and a doctor, who was among the audience, came running at once; but he could only confirm the unfortunate young woman's death.

News soon spread throughout the building. There was only one cry: "It's the Ladykiller again." But the dread was about to increase further. Suddenly, the electricity cut out, and a voice, that one would have said was broadcast through a very powerful loudspeaker, so formidable was it, boomed to the four corners of the hall where the horrified couples were pressed together,

"So will henceforth perish any woman found guilty of adultery."

Hardly had those words been uttered than the light returned to reveal a horrific sight…

Four more women were lying along the length of the pool which took up the centre of the hall. Lying on the slabs, they had also been struck down fatally.

When, the next day, Chantecoq learned of this massacre from the newspapers which had held up the presses in order to publish it, in spite of all his sang-froid, he gave a start of indignation and, jumping from his bed, he put on pyjamas and hastened down to his study. At once, he grabbed the phone and asked for Professor Courtil's number. He immediately came to the phone and, courteously, asked,

"Hello! My dear Monsieur Chantecoq, how can I be of service?"

Chantecoq answered, "Have you read the morning papers, my dear master?"

"I only just browsed through them."

"And did you see what happened in that dancehall?"

"I did. It's dreadful!"

"Isn't it? So, I was going to ask if you would intervene to restore the Ladykiller's new victims."

"It's quite difficult for me to intervene of my own volition."

"Do you give me free rein to act?"

"Of course."

"If, my dear master, you were called to the bedside of these unfortunates, would you accept to come and perform on them the same miracle you accomplished with Madame Barrois?"

"Absolutely, I promise you, and I even undertake not to leave my home. Just call me on the telephone, providing me with the address, and I'll come running."

"My most sincere thanks, my dear master."

"Yesterday, Monsieur Chantecoq, you entirely convinced me and I am completely of your mind; because I consider, as

94

you do, that however guilty these women may be, of whom many must have attenuating circumstances, the punishment inflicted on them is not in proportion with the fault they have committed."

"So it's agreed, my dear master?"

"Agreed, my dear detective!"

Chantecoq hung up the receiver, but only to pick it up once more and ask for the Baron d'Ormoix's number. It was a woman's voice who answered.

"Hello! Monsieur, who are you… what do you want?"

"I'm Monsieur Chantecoq, the detective. To whom do I have the honour of speaking?"

A voice broken by pain answered, "To the Marquise de Tallemard, mother of Baroness d'Ormoix."

Chantecoq replied, "May I, madame, have a meeting with you, as urgent as it is confidential?"

"On what subject, monsieur?"

"I can't tell you over the telephone; but all I can confirm is that I'm not one of those private detectives looking for a case. Full of pity, to the contrary, for your immense grief, I perhaps have in my hands the method to ease it and that's why I'm asking for a few minutes of your time, at once, if possible, while begging your pardon for troubling you in your despair and acting uniquely in the interest of her for whom you are weeping, and for all that are close to her."

The Marquise responded, "Monsieur Chantecoq, I know of you by name and by reputation; I therefore await you with confidence and I'll even add with hope."

"In one hour, madame, I'll have the honour of arriving with you."

According to his habit, the private detective found himself at the home of the Baroness d'Ormoix at the precise time he had announced.

The d'Ormoix family lived in a beautiful house on Rue Bassano, close to the Champs-Elysées. The house was in mourning. A profound atmosphere of tragic sadness reigned there.

Chantecoq was received at once by a butler with a serious face, and prim gestures, who introduced him immediately to the Marquise de Tallemard, who was in a boudoir whose curtains were drawn and which was lit by an electric lamp, diffused by a dark-coloured lampshade.

Giving every appearance of being a perfect man of the world, the policeman bowed respectfully to the Marquise, who, distraught with grief, was collapsed in a chair and seemed to no longer have the strength or the courage to make the slightest movement.

She spoke in a voice trembling with distress. "Monsieur, I was waiting for you with impatience. The telephone call you made to me earlier has lit in me the glimmer of a hope that I can't very well define, but which has comforted me a little in my immense grief."

"Madame," replied Chantecoq, "I would not like to rock you with too wonderful an illusion; I've always made it a principle, indeed, never to make engagements that I might be unable to accomplish and I've always preferred to try rather than to promise.

"Now, I'll explain the purpose of my visit, which isn't dictated by any personal interest, but solely by my profound desire to be useful not only to you, Marquise, but to everyone around you!

"I'll now relate to you, under a confidential seal, the reasons which dictated I must come."

Very favourably impressed by the bloodhound's language

and attitude, and aware in any case of his personal value and loyal probity, Madame de Tallemard replied. "Monsieur, you may speak in all security. As you seem to wish, no indiscretion will be committed by me. Everything you're going to say to me will remain a secret between us."

Relieved to find himself faced with a person who, in the middle of immense sorrow, was remaining so in control of herself, Chantecoq replied.

"Yesterday, madame, I declared merciless war on this enigmatic Ladykiller, who has already claimed so many victims, among which is counted - alas! - your daughter. And this is why.

"Yesterday, I became inarguably certain that a mysterious bandit had murdered a woman worthy of all respect. This is what happened. Following a very brief investigation that I carried out at once, after having established the evidence that this young person had remained entirely worthy of the love she inspired in her husband, I observed she was not dead, as everyone believed, but plunged deep into a lethargic slumber, or rather catalepsy, which made her resemble a corpse.

"I consulted a great scholar, largely unknown however, as are too many true geniuses. At my request, that scholar came to see the young woman, and succeeded in bringing her back to life.

"I don't want to get started, Madame, on a question which is none of my business, that's to say your daughter's private life and I'm happy to believe she too is an innocent victim."

"I thank you, monsieur," replied the Marquise de Tallemard with a voice full of poignant emotion, and she added at once, "You think, Monsieur Chantecoq, that the scholar of whom you just spoke, would agree to attempt this experiment on my poor daughter?"

"I'm better than convinced, I'm certain. I've only to telephone him, he will hurry over here. But, perhaps beforehand, it would be necessary to ask the opinion of the Baron d'Ormoix?"

"There's no need, monsieur," retorted the grand lady. "My son-in-law is not in Paris; I don't know where he is. He left several months ago and, since then, he's given us no sign of his whereabouts. He'll therefore learn of his wife's death through the newspapers.

"Ah! Monsieur Chantecoq, all this is lamentable and I'm a poor mother, very tested. That child was all I had in the world and here we are in the most painful circumstances imaginable."

"Madame, may I telephone Professor Courtil immediately?"

"Please do, monsieur," said the Marquise.

The king of detectives approached a telephone which was placed on a small table. He unhooked the receiver and asked for the scholar's number. He was put through after a brief delay and he contented himself simply by saying, "Hello! Chantecoq... I'd like you, my dear master, to come at once to 37, Rue de Bassano. I'll be waiting for you at the door... Yes, agreed... thank you... there's no need to tell you that everything will remain a secret."

He hung up the phone, returned to Madame de Talamard[8], who was sobbing, and said to her with a deferential and

_____

[8] Her name changed. I preserved the error (and it *is* an error, she changes back in a few paragraphs) because it's a clue that Bernède was, by this point in his career, dictating his books to secretaries. Tallemard and Talamard are practically homophonous in French.

sincere expression, "Perhaps all is not lost! I will ask you, madame, soon, when Professor Courtil arrives, to kindly make the necessary arrangements so that he and I are left alone in the dead woman's bedroom.

"Nothing simpler," declared Madame de Talamard. "My daughter is watched over by two nuns. I'll replace them until your friend arrives, then I'll leave you, as you wish, with my poor child."

The Marquise tried to stand. She looked so frail that Chantecoq instinctively offered her his arm; they went to the bedroom where the body of the Ladykiller's latest victim was on display.

While Madame de Tallemard murmured a few words to the nuns who, having crossed themselves devotedly, vanished like two shadows, Chantecoq looked at the young woman lying among the flowers.

She was also beautiful, very beautiful. A few hours previously, she must have exuded youth, gaiety, and life. But from his probing and penetrating gaze he at once had the impression that her face, much more than that of Marie-Louise Barrois, was reflecting death, and he didn't have that mysterious shock, that supernatural intuition, that he had felt in Marie-Louise's presence.

A kind of internal voice, to the contrary, appeared to warn him that, this time, the victim was not in catalepsy, but had truly succumbed. However, he didn't want to let his private thoughts show, and leaning over Madame de Tallemard, who had collapsed on one of the prie-dieus[9] that the nuns had vacated, he said to her in a low voice,

---

[9] Prie-dieu - a kind of prayer stool. The French term is better than the prosaic "kneeler".

"I'm going, madame, to watch for the professor's arrival."

"And I," murmured the poor woman feebly, "I'm going to pray to God, that he may permit a repeat of the miracle that you just described."

Chantecoq gave a simple nod of agreement, bowed before the mortal remains of Baroness d'Ormoix, and returned to the hallway where he met the butler, to whom he said,

"I'll return shortly with someone. In agreement with Madame the Marquise, I ask you to let this gentleman and I into the bedroom where Madame the Baroness d'Ormoix is lying."

The butler, a wily old Parisian, thought at once, "This is certainly someone from the police!"

He hastened to declare to Chantecoq, "That's agreed, monsieur. Madame the Marquise had given me orders to receive you at once. I'll therefore do just as you ask me."

He led the bloodhound to the door, and Chantecoq began to pace up and down the pavement.

Haunted by the thought that, this time, he had been in the presence of a corpse, he thought,

"This is endlessly curious. Ah! Could it be that the Ladykiller learned I was involved in this case and, thanks to Professor Courtil's intervention, I succeeded in resuscitating one of his victims?

"For that he'd need to possess channels of communication of a disconcerting rapidity. In the end, I'm perhaps mistaken; it could be after all that the Baroness d'Ormoix is no more dead than Madame Barrois, and it's useless to give myself over to any conjecture, before Professor Courtil has come and pronounced his verdict."

Chantecoq lit a cigarette and had finished smoking it

100

when a taxi stopped in front of 37 Rue Bassano. A door opened, and Professor Courtil climbed out of the cab.

Chantecoq went towards him and said simply, "Pay the fare now, I'll take you back in my car."

The scholar paid the driver and must have given him a good tip, because while he didn't receive any change, he also didn't receive any invective.

Chantecoq, taking the professor's arm, said to him in a curt voice, "Everything's arranged with the family, an old and distinguished mother whose grief is frightful… You just have to follow me."

Chantecoq kept himself from communicating his personal impressions to his collaborator, so as not to influence him and, after having rung at the door, they entered the house.

As he had agreed, the butler led Chantecoq and his companion straight to the bedroom. On seeing them, Madame de Tallemard stood and, without having the strength to utter a word, she responded to the greeting Professor Courtil gave her with a look so expressive that it would have melted a heart of stone, and she withdrew, her shoulders bowed and wiping with her handkerchief her poor eyes, which were red with tears.

Professor Courtil approached the baroness's body which he examined at length. He gave a little shake of his head; then, turning back to the king of detectives, he said to him,

"I'm rather afraid I'll be unable to reanimate this unfortunate; I perceive already on her face some brown stains, very light, it's true, but nonetheless early signs of the decomposition process. No matter! I'll try the experiment all the same; if it doesn't succeed, it won't be my fault, and, this time, the Ladykiller will really have killed."

The scholar carried out on Madame Véra d'Ormoix the same operation as on Marie-Louise.

When it was finished, replacing his instruments in his pouch, the scholar said to Chantecoq,

"Now we can only wait."

After fifteen minutes, no signs of life were revealed.

"Sadly," opined the professor, "my first impression was correct. There's nothing to be done. Either we arrived too late, or the murderer used a toxin which, this time, killed in a single stroke."

"Let's wait a few more moments?" Chantecoq asked.

"If you wish."

Five minutes passed, then the bedroom door opened, revealing the Marquise's silhouette.

Her gaze, which was no longer obscured by tears and which was shining, instead, with a feverish light, was directed, pleading and anguished, towards the two men who were continuing to observe in silence the young woman, lying among the flowers.

She understood at once that the attempt had not succeeded; and, in a broken voice, she said,

"She's dead, isn't she?"

Professor Courtil responded simply, "Alas, madame..."

Chantecoq, looking pained, said, "Forgive me, madame, for provoking a vain hope in you."

"I don't blame you, monsieur. Rather I'll remember only the generous intent which guided you."

Two silent shadows returned to the bedroom: it was the nuns, who, once more, were kneeling on the prie-dieu. Madame de Tallemard, her strength exhausted, fell on to an armchair, and the vigil began again.

8 MÉTÉOR AND SCHOLASTIC

When the king of detectives entrusted a mission to his secretary, he, as readers who have made their way through *The Mystery of the Blue Train, The Haunted House, The Aviator's Crime, Zapata, The Amorous Ogre, The Père-Lachaise Ghost, Condemned to Death,* etc, etc, will have observed with what zeal and skill, he acquitted himself.

Assimilating more and more of the methods of his master towards whom he professed an admiration that was as deep as it was sincere, Météor began by establishing a plan not rigid but, to the contrary, susceptible to all modifications that might be necessitated by unforeseen circumstances, such as are always encountered in the course of police enquiries.

He forced himself, at first, to envisage the situation with an absolute sense of the realities and rigorously forbade his imagination from lending its input before he was informed exactly on the terrain on which he was going to be working.

In the event, he began by rereading the stenography of the conversation that his master had the day before with Monsieur Maurice Barrois.

Then, with a few brief and judicious notes, he summarised those words that he had exchanged with his boss.

All that, obviously, had only a very indirect link with Professor Courtil. However Météor had understood the necessity of being in full possession of all the elements which preceded the king of detective's negotiations with the scholar.

He had this judicious thought: "As the boss asked me to look into this man's past secretly, to find out why there's a gap in his life and learn what this man did during that time, it therefore follows that he's not entirely sure of him. Who's to say that he might not even suspect him of being…"

But hardly had that idea blossomed in his mind than Météor, at once, said to himself, "My friend, let's put the brakes on quick; or we're going to get carried away and without doubt on the wrong track, which would be lamentable. However, as my boss always recommends, I only have to follow his directives and I no more have the right to discard them than I do to exceed them.

"So I've just got to think how I'll conduct myself in order to get close to this lady Scholastic. From the little my boss told me, she sounds like a Cerberus who can't be easy to tame!

"If she was still young and not too ugly, one could try to court her a bit by introducing oneself to her under the guise of a rich American or a gallant aviator. But it appears, as the vulgar expression would have it, that she's rather 'grated cheese'. So another approach is needed. Before beginning, let's take a look at her!"

Météor went out, took a taxi, and stopped at the entrance to Rue Bonaparte.

After having paid the driver, he went straight to 37 Rue Bonaparte and walked up and down in front of the building's entrance.

It wasn't long before he saw an old lady coming out, a shopping basket in her hand. She decisively resembled the portrait Chantecoq had made of her.

Météor gave a crooked smile, which meant that he was happy.

Then, without taking a break, he went into the house and asked the concierge, in the most casual manner, "Madame, could you tell me please, on which floor does Professor Courtil live?"

"On the second, to the right."

"Thank you, madame," said Météor. He was about to leave, when she said to him, "There's no point in troubling yourself, monsieur, there's no one at home. The professor left in the early afternoon, and his maid just left to go shopping."

"Thank you, madame," replied Météor. "You're very kind. But tell me, Monsieur Courtil's maid might not be long in coming home?"

"Oh! I wouldn't advise you to wait for her, because her absence can be rather long."

"Oh, really!"

"Every day, at this time, having done her shopping, she heads to Saint-Sulpice, where she spends at least an hour at prayer."

And without Météor needing to ask for the slightest clarification, she continued with a volubility and abundance that demonstrated she was blessed with the gift of speech and was ceaselessly ready to make use of it.

"Madame Scholastic is more than pious, she's a bigot. As

105

for me, I don't have many beliefs, but I make it a principle to respect those of other people.

"I don't prevent anyone from going to Mass and I don't want to be forced to go myself. My husband is like me; that's to tell you we're not unpleasant people."

"Madame," Météor complimented her, anxious to keep himself in the concierge's good graces, "it's enough for me to see you and hear you, to be certain that you are kindness itself."

At such a direct compliment, the concierge blushed with pleasure; because she was not immune to flattery; and, at once, she replied, giving free rein to her garrulous nature,

"Madame Scholastic isn't a bad person. Far from it! Only, for her, it's only priests who count. Doubtless because she had a priest for a son…"

"In Paris?" Chantecoq's disciple asked insidiously.

"Oh no!" replied his companion. "He was a vicar in Brittany, in Vannes. Would you like me to show you his picture on a postcard? Madame Scholastic gave it to me!"

"With pleasure," declared Météor.

The concierge, who answered to the name of Madame Dugazou, went to the back of the room, opened a drawer, took out the portrait in question and brought it to the detective's secretary, who looked at it without appearing to attach the slightest importance to it.

"Oh!" he said, returning the image to its owner, "He was a vicar in Vannes…"

"Yes," declared the concierge, "At the church of Saint-Paterne."

Mechanically, Météor turned the postcard over, while saying, "He looks very pleasant. He has a very kind face. He must be a good man."

And he read the few lines written on the back of the card addressed to Madame Scholastic.

Dear mother, today is the anniversary of my father's death; I'm therefore going to say a Mass for him. I think about you a lot and I send you my kindest thoughts. My colleague and friend Abbot Vergeon is going to Paris in around a month. He will come and say hello on my behalf, because I've spoken to him so much about you, he would like to meet you.

I send you all my filial thoughts and best wishes.

Your son,

Pierre-Jean Mériadeck.

Météor checked the letter's date and noticed it had been around fifteen days since it must have reached its destination.

He returned the postcard to Madame Dugazou, while saying to her, "Obviously, Madame Scholastique has maybe an excess of devotion. But the praise her son pays her seems to establish that she's a very honest and worthy woman."

"That I will agree with," cried the concierge. "And devoted to her master! She has been in his service for more than thirty years. Her husband was the valet in the house. It appears Professor Courtil is much richer than he looks!

"Oh! That one, there's a phenomenon! What a number! He doesn't appear proud, and surely isn't, as he wants only to take care of the poor and he cares for everyone in sight. But, as to getting a single word out of him, it's as though you're asking the Eiffel Tower to transform itself into Sacré-Coeur.

"Sometimes, he passes right by you without saying hello. He can't be judged for it: he's like scholars, they think only about what's going on in their heads. So I don't even pay attention to what he does say.

107

"Madame Scholastic, who comes to chat with us from time to time - because he never speaks to her - was telling me again yesterday evening that it's not even worth the trouble to cook for him properly, as he's incapable of distinguishing a nasty burnt chop from a good steak and spuds.

"He eats in order to eat, he drinks in order to drink. Outside of his patients, he receives no one, he goes nowhere, he's always plunged in his books. She must truly have devotion engraved on her heart to stay in the service of such a loon."

Madame Dugazou was going to continue her confidences, but Météor doubtless judged he had learned enough, because, cutting sharply across the verbal torrent from the attendant, he said,

"Thank you so much, madame, for your friendly welcome; I'll come back at another time."

After having bowed politely to Madame Dugazou, he withdrew, without giving her time to launch into another tirade.

Quickly he took another taxi and returned to Avenue de Verzy.

Twenty minutes later he left again, dressed in ecclesiastical clothes which gave him every appearance of a young provincial priest.

The camouflage was complete. Météor had forgotten nothing, not even his prayer book.

He had found the costume and its accessories in Chantecoq's inexhaustible repertoire of outfits; as the born actor he was, he had added the look, attitude, unremarkable features to give the character he was playing every appearance of an authentic vicar.

Still in a taxi, he returned to Rue Bonaparte and stopped

outside number 37.

Passing, he glanced inside the concierge's lodge, who was busy preparing her evening meal. He therefore judged it pointless to disturb her and he promptly climbed the two flights of stairs which led to the professor's apartment.

He rang discreetly; no answer.

"Damn it!" Météor thought. "Could it be that she's still in ecstasies before the Holy Virgin's altar?"

However he seemed to hear, as he pressed his ear against the door, the sound of shuffling slippers, coming from the apartment.

He rang again a little louder. Still nothing!

"How daft I am!" he said to himself. "I'd completely forgotten old mother Scholastic's deaf."

For the third time he rang, violently, the broken bell.

This time, Scholastic heard and opened the door.

On the sight of this young priest, with a candid face and onctuous mannerisms, the poor old woman joined her hands together as if she had seen God Himself appear to her.

Very satisfied with this effect on she from whom he wanted to get as much information as possible, Météor, imperturbable, introduced himself, raising his voice, "I'm Reverend Vergeon."

Scholastic's face was beaming. "Reverend Vergeon," she repeated, parting her hands, "my son's friend? You're welcome, I wasn't expecting you so soon!"

Météor explained, "Dear madame, I had to bring forward my trip by a few days. I arrived this morning, and I couldn't delay bringing you my best wishes, as well as news of your son."

"How good you are!" cried Madame Scholastic. "I can't leave you in the hallway like this."

109

And, closing the front door which had stayed open, she said, "Would you care to come through into the lounge?"

Météor excused himself, "I wouldn't want to impose, nor disturb Professor Courtil."

Scholastic said, "The professor isn't here, and from what he told me, he won't be returning home straight away. Anyway, he'll be very happy to see you. He is my boy's godfather; he loves him a lot; as you're his colleague and his friend, I'm sure that, although he might not be on very friendly terms with the world, he'll offer you the warmest welcome."

And, opening the waiting room door for him, she added, "Come in then, monsieur; I beg you, make yourself at home."

She offered a seat to the visitor and remained standing; but with a great deal of deference, the fake Reverend Vergeon, said to her, "Please."

The old servant sat on the edge of a chair; and, while considering her visitor with a tender air, she said, "It's a pleasure to make your acquaintance. It's very curious, I received quite a long letter from my son just this morning, and he didn't talk at all about your arrival."

That allegation, which could have been a problem for many others, didn't seem to embarrass Chantecoq's pupil in the least.

In the most natural tone, he said, "Nothing extraordinary about that, madame, because it was only yesterday evening, around six o'clock, that the cathedral curate told me I was leaving for Paris. Doubtless, my colleague's letter was written and in the post before Monsieur the Curate communicated his decision to me."

"Ah! That must be it."

110

There was a brief silence. Météor took the opportunity to cast a quick look around him, and Madame Scholastic continued. "So, my little one's well?"

At once, she added, "Forgive me for calling him that, but it's a habit that I have from his birth, and I believe that if I'm still living when he's sixty years old, I'd still call him my little one."

This sincere demonstration of maternal affection couldn't fail to make an excellent impression on Météor; because he was blessed with a very good heart and, during previous investigations, had often had to impose silence on himself so as not to let himself be carried away by dangerous pity.

However, his conscience reassured him at once. He wasn't trying to fool this lady at all; he simply wanted to obtain from her lips the details which were of interest to his boss and, without causing any problems for this woman, to accomplish his professional duty to uncover the truth, in the interests of justice.

Restoring his composure completely, he continued, "I understand, madame, that you should be so tenderly attached to your son. He entirely deserves it, because his is one of the noblest hearts that I've ever encountered in this world."

"Isn't he, though?" cried Scholastic, delighted.

Météor continued. "I don't need to tell you how much, for his part, he is tenderly attached to you. He has only one dream: that's to be named as curate as soon as possible, even in a little parish, so as to call you to come and live nearby. It weighs on him heavily to tell himself that you're in a situation and that, above, all, you're perhaps not always very happy."

"Oh!" said Scholastic. "The professor is very good to me; never does he make any reproaches to me, no reprimands; I might even say that he let's me do whatever I want. The fact

111

is, he doesn't talk much."

"That's what Reverend Pierre told me."

"He must have told you also that it's not entirely his fault. It seems Monsieur Courtil has been most unfortunate."

"Your son also told me he was a very great scholar."

"For sure," the servant emphasised. "I even believe there aren't many in France who come as high as his ankle; that's why his colleagues made him the victim of so many attacks."

Sighing, Scholastic added, "If only it had been just that, my God! He would have fought, he would even have triumphed; he's a man who has not only science within him, but also a will such as one doesn't often see. Pierre has perhaps told you…"

She stopped with a questioning expression. Skillfully Météor replied, "Your son has indeed alluded to certain private sorrows."

As though she was feeling a satisfaction or rather a comfort in speaking with someone she judged capable of understanding her, the old servant continued.

"You can't imagine how my master suffered! To you, I can say it; you're accustomed to receiving confidences and keeping secrets. Well! There was a terrible one in the professor's life; I know it; my son knows it too."

And lowering her voice, leaning towards the fake Reverend Vergeon, who, his eyes lowered, his face grave, reflective, had the exact attitude of a priest preparing to hear a confession, Scholastic, who would have chopped off her own leg sooner than speak a word on this subject, even to one of her closest friends, said with a convinced tone,

"To you I can say everything because a priest, it's not the same thing and, at least, you'll be one more to pray that the poor man doesn't end his life too unhappily and that he ends up not by forgetting his misfortune, but at least by consoling himself for it, by ceasing to be an unbeliever and becoming a good Christian."

"Speak, madame," invited the fake vicar with an admirable air of compunction.

Scholastic continued.

"Professor Courtil married, in Nancy, a young woman who was very rich and very pretty. That was a marriage not of interest, but of inclination.

"So long as they both lived in that town, where I was in their service, as well as my poor dead husband, the household went marvellously and, when they came to settle in Paris, I noticed that after a certain period, things weren't going so well. Oh! Not on the part of Monsieur, who took every care for Madame, but rather on the part of Madame, who was always going out, visiting, for walks, and no longer paying any attention to her soul.

"At first, Monsieur said nothing, but it was easy to notice he was suffering greatly. Soon, disputes broke out between them. I never had the habit of listening at doors, because I'm discreet and I've always been a little hard of hearing but, I'm sure they weren't in agreement!

"My poor deceased husband, who was a valet and heard more clearly than I, told me Monsieur was reproaching Madame for going out too often on her own, for not telling him where she was going and, above all, for refusing to go out for walks with him.

"That all lasted at least three or four years, when one evening, he found Madame, lying in her bedroom, at the foot of her bed.

"He called us quickly; we believed at first that she had only fainted, but she was dead, stone cold dead, and three

113

days later she was buried in Nancy in her family tomb.

"Monsieur displayed such violent grief that, for two weeks, we believed he was going to die; but his robust constitution took over; then, he decided he would go to live in the provinces and withdraw from the world entirely.

"I offered to take him to our region in Brittany where we would help him lead a very quiet life. He didn't have an enormous fortune, because, although his family had instituted him as sole heir, he insisted on restoring to the family of the deceased the full dowry he had received.

"As he had sold some patents, some inventions to some great houses of pharmaceutical products, he wasn't short. I've not seen his accounts, but I've an idea he must have around one hundred thousand francs in annuities.

"As he doesn't spend anything to speak of for his personal use, I'm quite sure he puts the money to one side and gives it to the unfortunates, which is more likely; because, beneath his cold, glacial exterior, he is kindness personified!

"Finally we left with him for our region, in Rosporden where he rented a house with a large garden. He built a kind of workshop, which he called his laboratory; there, he locked himself away from nine o'clock in the morning until noon and from one o'clock in the afternoon until seven o'clock in the evening and was working, working... to forget, of course.

"But I believe that didn't happen; because, sometimes, I surprised him in the act of wiping his eyes, as though he had just been crying and wanted to hide his tears from us.

"That lasted for years, until the day, four years ago, when Monsieur came to Paris to move into this apartment. One year later, I lost my poor man. I remained all alone, with my boss. He no longer has anyone but me in the world, and I

114

wouldn't want to abandon him, not for millions."

"That's very fine on your part," answered the fake Reverend Vergeon. "I can only, madame, congratulate you on your devotion, because, above all since the death of your poor husband, life can't have been very pleasant for you."

"Oh! I have my son to console me. I don't see him very often, but I think of him all the time. He writes me such beautiful letters that it seems to me I can hear him speaking. I reply to him as best I can, and we communicate at a distance like that.

"Anyway, for nothing in the world would I want to leave Monsieur all alone. I have the consolation of having my son during his holidays, which he comes to spend close to me, and there's always that…

"From one end of the year to the other, I live in the hope that he's going to come. That stops me from getting bored, because I'm all alone here…"

"You must not see many people."

"Other than clients, I never see anyone. Anyway, it was absolutely the same sort of thing when we were in Rosporden. Monsieur never uttered a word to anyone, he never went out; he contented himself with walking in his garden, when the weather was fine.

"Many times, my husband and I, we asked him if he wanted to go on a trip to the countryside as far as the sea.

"He answered no, shaking his head sadly. Then we didn't dare insist, because when we spoke of that, he was even sadder than before!

"The truth is Monsieur never recovered from Madame's death, and he'll never recover from it."

Météor clearly felt he had learned all he wished to know,

because he stood up and said, "Madame, I beg your pardon for having held you up for so long."

Scholastic declared, "I'm very happy, actually, that you came to pay me a visit. It's allowed me to talk about my son with you, and as you'll certainly see him sooner than I will, you'll be good enough to tell him that I'm well and I'm always thinking of him."

"Madame, this task will be accomplished," replied Météor.

And he respectfully clasped the hand that the old servant held out to him, before she led him to the door, while renewing her recommendations with regard to her son. Météor returned to the street, jumped into a taxi and was taken back to Allée de Verzy, to Chantecoq's home. But the king of detectives had not yet returned. Météor took the opportunity to undress, remove his makeup, and return to his usual appearance, and awaited his boss's return.

By eight o'clock, the great bloodhound still hadn't appeared. Météor began to worry somewhat.

He went to find Pierre Gautrais, and asked him if he hadn't received, in the course of the afternoon, some communication from his master, warning him he wouldn't be dining or that he would be home late.

The valet explained that no, he had not, but there were no grounds to worry about it.

At half past eight, Chantecoq was still not there. A terrible thought suddenly arose in Météor's mind, a suspicion which was translated into these words, spoken in a low voice,

"Just so long as the Ladykiller hasn't learned the boss is on his tail and managed to give him a fatal jab!"

He tried to reassure himself, saying, "If such a tragedy had struck, we'd already know about it."

Suddenly, a joyful voice rang out close to him. "Oh yes, we'd know all about it, my brave lad."

Météor shivered with relief; his boss had entered the study and, approaching his secretary, he said, putting his hand amicably on his shoulder, "Do you imagine, by any chance, that I'm no longer capable of defending myself?"

"Oh no, boss," Météor riposted energetically, "You've never been so on form. Only, here's the thing, I've so much affection for you that, when we're apart, my imagination beats the charm, and I always imagine a whole heap of things."

"You're wrong, my dear boy," replied the great bloodhound. "You must know that I'm a man who takes precautions. I never set off lightly… The fear you had, I had it too and I arranged to protect myself from all jabs, even from a bee… I'll explain soon because it's also necessary that you be as protected as I am."

"Boss, you always think of everything!"

Chantecoq, lightly, declared, "I believe it's time to sit down to dinner; because Marie-Jeanne's fricot stew must have waited long enough. After dinner, we'll return here; you'll give me the results of your investigation and I'll bring you up to date with everything I did this afternoon."

Chantecoq pressed a button for an electric bell which communicated directly with the kitchen. It was the prearranged signal to warn the cordon bleu that the feasting hour had struck.

Chantecoq and his secretary sat down at the table and did justice to the excellent consommé, omelette, slices of cold meat and to the salad which were served to them. Nothing to speak of was left of the fruit tart that was brought to them by way of dessert.

During this meal, Chantecoq made no allusion to the case at hand. Météor diagnosed from this that he was very satisfied with the results he'd obtained and he rejoiced at that himself. Once the last mouthful had been swallowed, Chantecoq returned to his study with his collaborator and, sitting on an armchair, he lit his pipe peacefully and said to Météor,

"The floor is yours."

With a fidelity verging on the stenographic, Chantecoq's disciple gave his exact, complete, and detailed account of his encounter with old Scholastic.

Generally, when he had finished, his boss would ask him, "What did you conclude from that?"

This time, the great private detective, who had listened with the utmost attention, remained completely silent.

Worried, Météor wondered, "Could I, by any chance, have missed the mark? Did I botch my mission? The boss doesn't seem at all happy…"

Météor was mistaken, because suddenly Chantecoq spoke up. "Now I'm fixed on several little points which were frustrating me somewhat. Yes, it's indeed as I thought. Only, it's going to be hard, very hard even, and I wonder how I'm going to catch him in the act; because he must always be on guard… In the end, we shall see."

And standing up, he added, "Now, little Météor, it's my turn to tell you what I've done. As you played an important role in this case, it's essential you're up to date with everything."

Météor's eyes shone in an intense fashion. The fact was that his boss's last words had plunged him so much deeper into a joyful mood as they were inarguable proof that the king of detectives wasn't hesitating to place his trust in him.

Chantecoq continued. "This morning, I went to the home of the Baroness d'Ormoix, one of the Ladykiller's latest victims. I succeeded in seeing her on her deathbed and, although I had the impression or rather the intuition that I had a cadaver in front of me, I didn't hesitate to summon Professor Courtil.

"He, just as he promised, came running at my call. He told me at once that he had the same instinct as I. Nevertheless he conducted on Baroness d'Ormoix the same experiment as on Marie-Louise Barrois. Unfortunately, it didn't succeed. The poor woman was truly dead.

"From there, we visited in succession the four other ladies who succumbed that same evening in the famous Champs-Elysées dancehall and we observed that it was impossible to restore them to life.

"All those missions took us a great deal of time. I had to drive Professor Courtil back home, and that's why I've returned home so late.

"Now I would be curious to know what deduction you are drawing from these new facts, of which, I'm sure, the gravity will not have escaped you."

"Boss, I confess to you frankly that I would prefer you to tell me your opinion on all that rather than offering you my own."

"Why?"

"Because I'm afraid of saying something daft."

"What do you know of it? You can, to the contrary, through your reflections, draw my attention on to some points that I might not yet have studied. And then, how would I judge your progress if, from time to time, I didn't make you sit a little exam?"

"There, boss, you're absolutely right, and I no longer have the right to have my ear tweaked. What I think, ah! It's very simple: it's just as you already guessed, the Ladykiller was warned that you had succeeded in reviving one of his victims through Professor Courtil and, that being the case, he judged it pointless to complicate their torture, having them buried alive, and judged it preferable to send them at once into eternity."

"Up to this point," replied Chantecoq, "we're in complete agreement. Now, continue."

"Boss, I'm very embarrassed. Now, I find nothing to say to you, I'm floundering; I must think…"

Chantecoq, smiling, asked, "You weren't surprised the Ladykiller was so quickly aware of Madame Marie-Louise Barrois's resurrection?"

"That's it exactly, boss, that's what I was in the process of telling myself. Indeed, barely more than a few hours passed between the attack of which Madame Barrois failed to be the victim, and those at the dancehall on Avenue Champs-Elysées."

"Good," said the great bloodhound with an approving nod, "and after?"

"After? Damn! Boss, that's what's still puzzling me… however, there is something which troubles me, and certainly it's a question you must have asked yourself. How could the Ladykiller know for sure that the women he strikes have cheated on their husbands?"

"Obviously," Chantecoq conceded, "that's a very curious and very troubling point, which would seem to prove that our mysterious bandit has numerous informants and, yet, I hesitate to believe that, my flair tells me that this scoundrel works alone; however, as you said so well just now, my brave lad, there's no point embarrassing ourselves in the spotlight. The most important thing isn't how the Ladykiller informs himself of the guilt of those he intends to sacrifice. He alone can tell us all that; the important thing is to find out who he is and, above all, to have such clear evidence of his guilt that he will be unable to escape the guillotine or the asylum.

"Criminal or madman, we absolutely must prevent, as soon as possible, the sinister functions attributed to him."

"Boss, your words are golden. Only, that's the thing, that's what I still don't see, how can we discover or trap him?"

"At first," retorted the detective, "it's a case of proceeding by deduction. For that, we would first need to know if, since this morning at ten o'clock until nine o'clock this evening, the Ladykiller claimed any other victims?"

"Nothing easier," declared Météor. "You just have to telephone your friend Monsieur Lereni, the new chief commissioner, and I'm sure he'll be pleased to give you an update."

"I thought of that," replied the king of detectives, "but I wouldn't want the state police to learn that I'm involved in this business. I prefer to wait and read the newspapers tomorrow, which will provide full details of this matter."

"As always boss, you're right," replied the young secretary.

And as if he felt the need to refresh his brain, Chantecoq said to his pupil, "If we went into the billiards room, we could indulge in a few rounds of cannons. That would give our grey matter a bit of a rest and we'd be able to stretch our legs."

"With pleasure, boss," the excellent Météor agreed.

Hardly had they spoken those words when there was a

knock at the door.

"Come in," said Chantecoq.

Pierre Gautrais appeared. He was carrying on a platter a card which he gave to the great bloodhound. He took it and read the name written on the card.

"Ah! Now that's very good!" It's just like the proverb, "Speak of the devil and he shall appear."

And turning towards Météor, he said, "Let's put aside our game of billiards for another time; because I've just received my great friend Lereni, who sent this card along to me."

"Now that's funny!"

Chantecoq replied, "As we never know what might happen, and although I have absolute faith in this dear commissioner's loyalty, I'll ask you to take up your usual observation post, get hold of your notebook, your pencil, and take down in shorthand the whole conversation that takes place between that excellent civil servant and I."

"Understood, boss," said the secretary.

And turning on his heel, Météor appeared to vanish into thin air.

Chantecoq ordered Pierre Gautrais:

"Show Monsieur Lereni in." While the valet went to carry out his orders, Chantecoq murmured, "I suspect, or rather I know why this dear friend has come to pay me a visit. He believes he'll astonish me. Ah well! I believe that it's I who will surprise him even more… In any case, if he's coming to ask for information, I'll give it to him with pleasure, but I rather believe it's him who will be furnishing it to me."

9 THE TWO POLICEMEN

As our readers have been able to observe in the course of this tale, as in several others, the author of these lines, charged with making known to the public the great deeds of a private detective, has always been the first to pay homage to the official state police.

Never has he passed up an opportunity to put in lights the professional values of its representatives, or to pay homage to the courage, to the probity, to the honourable sentiments which characterise, excepting rare exceptions, those precious auxiliaries of society.

Furthermore, we have never wanted to confuse our friend Chantecoq with certain chiefs from those corridors who, founded on the specious pretexts of research in the interest of family security, are much more often real crooks, because as much as the private police, when represented by honest people - and that corporation counts more than might perhaps be believed - deserves our esteem and our sympathy, as much, when it has for directors of tainted individuals, who seek to profit from misfortune, errors, and from the vices of our contemporaries, it must be hounded without pity and suppressed as a breeding ground of contagion.

May we be pardoned for this declaration of principle; it is absolutely necessary to establish before the scene that we're about to reproduce.

Indeed, if Chantecoq represented the ideal private detective, Monsieur Lereni was, for his part, the very personification of the perfect police officer.

Aged around forty years or so, gifted with aptitudes and professional knowledge that had carried him irresistibly to the highly important functions that he occupied, with rare distinction and true success, Monsieur Lereni was, furthermore, an extremely courteous and cultivated man.

Very composed, he never let himself get angry and he never even became irritated when he found himself in the presence of facts or acts which could have inspired a legitimate reaction of humour or even the most reasonable irritation.

In that, he greatly resembled Chantecoq, under whose orders he had served when the king of detectives occupied an important position in Sûreté générale.

The pupil retained for his master, to whom he owed everything, deep gratitude and sincere friendship.

For his part, Chantecoq appreciated him greatly and always maintained with him a relationship imprinted with the most frank cordiality.

Sometimes, when Monsieur Lereni had to elucidate an embarrassing case, he came for advice from the man who initiated him in the difficult art of pursuing wrongdoers and arresting them.

So the great bloodhound had been somewhat surprised, on observing that on the subject of this case of the

Ladykiller, one of the most extraordinary and the most arduous which had popped up for many years, Monsieur Lereni had not yet come to find him. And he said to himself,

"For him to have made his mind up so late, it must be that something new or unusual has happened… as long as…"

Chantecoq stopped thinking.

Monsieur Lereni stepped towards him, his hand outstretched.

"Good evening, my dear master," he began. "Forgive me for disturbing you at such an hour."

While exchanging a vigorous handshake with him, Chantecoq replied, "You know very well, my dear friend, that you've always been and will always be welcome."

"I know," replied the director of the judicial police, "and I greatly regret that time is too short for me to make more frequent visits, because, every time I see you and am able to talk with you, even if just for a few moments, I always learn something…"

"My dear Lereni," Chantecoq, always modest, was self-effacing. "I assure you that you're exaggerating…"

"Not at all," protested the official policeman. "But don't believe that I'm just here to pay you compliments… no… I've come to consult you…"

"On the subject of the case of the Ladykiller?"

"As I came to realise a long time ago, it's impossible to hide anything from you." Lereni smiled. "I would have done so much sooner, had I not been assured that you were completely disinterested in the case…"

"That was exactly the situation." Chantecoq acknowledged.

"But no longer…"

"Precisely."

The explanations were clear and simple between two men of such a temperament and such a character, who professed for each other, more than solid affection, but an esteem which was doubled in the younger with deference and sincere admiration.

Monsieur Lereni replied at once.

"I learned yesterday, thanks to the aid of a scholar whose name was unknown to me until today…"

"Professor Courtil?"

"The very same. You accomplished the miracle of resurrecting one of the Ladykiller's victims."

"As always, my dear director, you're admirably informed," declared the king of detectives, without the slightest irony. "But what you perhaps didn't know is that today we were much less fortunate, and this dreadful bandit's five latest victims, that's to say those killed yesterday evening in the dancehall on Champs-Elysées, were, alas, truly dead, and it was impossible to reanimate them."

"I knew that also," Monsieur Lereni affirmed, with frankness.

"My compliments…"

"Don't think that I had you followed."

"Had you done so, you would have been entirely within your rights…"

The director of the judicial police said, "Obliged to investigate the latest deaths as well as the preceding ones, it was my inspectors who revealed your intervention in their reports to me, which I was no longer expecting…"

"If I entered in the dance," declared Chantecoq, "it was

to answer the prayers of Madame Marie-Louise Barrois's father-in-law, who wanted to know the truth, the full truth, behind his daughter-in-law's mysterious death.

"I quickly found proof that the Ladykiller, this time, had not struck down an unfaithful woman, but, instead, the most pure and the most loving of wives. Then, on contemplating the victim, I had the intuition she was still alive. My flair…"

"Let's rather say your genius!"

"Well. I remember that there lived on Rue Bonaparte a doctor, unknown to science, or rather to scholars, who had succeeded in rousing people believed to be dead, but who were only sleeping. He was a character…"

"I already procured his pedigree," declared Lereni. "At first glance, he appeared interesting to me."

"Indeed," agreed Chantecoq, without insisting further.

And, picking up his tale, he continued. "I went to his home. I asked him to come with me to Madame Barrois. At first he hesitated. Then, he gave in to my arguments. But I'll stop there, because, from what you just told me, you know as much about that as I do."

"I wish I did!" Lereni joked with a smile which was somewhat tainted with melancholy.

"So," exclaimed Chantecoq, "you imagine that I've uncovered the Ladykiller?"

"No, but I'm sure you're on his trail."

"I would be lying if I told you otherwise," the king of detectives acknowledged.

And, with a spontaneous gesture, he added, "If it bothers you in the slightest that I'm looking into this sinister individual, tell me frankly, dear friend, and I'll immediately stop thinking about him. It will be easy for me, as I'm not charged with any particular mandate; and if, after Madame Barrois's resurrection, I continue to look into this case, it's solely for humanitarian reasons."

"I recognise you there, my dear master."

"You see, Loreni," replied Chantecoq, "when one has money and renown, when one still feels young and can easily take a gilded retirement, one is often tempted to withdraw from circulation. But, suddenly, the love of the job grabs you again. One continues to work as a dilettante, and also because your conscience engages you not to be disinterested in certain problems which, by remaining insoluble, risk great harm to society. But be assured, my dear Lereni, I don't want to cause you any trouble, by acting, in this circumstance, at the margins of the police. I'm ready, instead, to retire, to back down before you and even to reveal to you everything I know."

"Master, there I again recognise your admirable generosity."

"No, I'm logical with myself. We're both pursuing the same goal."

"So?" Lereni asked. "Let's pursue it together…"

Chantecoq fell silent. He took his pipe, filled it, lit it. Lereni was watching him, wondering, "What is he going to decide? Have I offended him without meaning to?"

Finally, Chantecoq, after having taken several lungfuls of smoke, replied. "Before responding, my dear friend, I've examined my own thoughts and I'm asking you truly and amicably, yes or no: do you really need me?"

With an accent of undeniable sincerity, Monsieur Lereni answered. "I'm convinced, my dear master, that, alone, you can unravel this enigma. As for me, I renounce it."

"Why?"

"Because, to get hold of this bandit or this madman, you'd need to be blessed with a true gift of divination which I lack and you, you possess to the highest degree."

Chantecoq laughed. "Why not come right out and say I'm a wizard?"

"You have all the gifts of one, all the faculties," replied the director of judicial police.

"So, you believe that in the Middle Ages I would have been burned at the stake?"

"No, my dear master, because you could only ever have been a benevolent wizard and I believe the Church, if you had agreed to bow before its doctrine, would have considered you to be God's envoy on this Earth, in order to accomplish some miracles down here and that it would not have neglected, after your death, to catalogue you among the number of its saints."

"Saint Chantecoq," cried the great bloodhound, bursting with laughter. "There's a name that Saint Peter certainly wouldn't much have wanted to hear echoing in his ears! But let's talk seriously and return to the question."

Seriously, the king of detectives intoned, "Desperate at your failure to discover the Ladykiller, and knowing I was on the case, you come to ask not for leads, but for my collaboration?"

"That's it exactly."

"I have no reason to refuse it, and less to you than to any other; and I am disposed to agree, but on two conditions."

"What are they, my dear master?"

"The first is that you will immediately send home all the inspectors and agents that you've sent into the field and act yourself only following my absolute directives. This process is doubtless going to seem somewhat dictatorial to you."

"Not at all," protested the director of judicial police, "and I subscribe very gladly to this first condition."

Chantecoq gave an approving nod. Then he continued. "The second, is that our dealings remain completely secret. Beyond you and I, it's agreed that no one will know, if I succeed, that it was I who arrested the Ladykiller."

"May I, my dear master," asked Lereni, "ask you why?"

"My dear friend," Chantecoq declared, "I'm not in the habit of taking credit for the favours that I do for friends."

The director held out his hand.

"Never," he cried, "I'll never forget what you're doing for me. Without you, I was in distinct danger of losing my superiors' confidence. The papers begin to make allusions to the slow work of the police force. In certain cabaret shows in Montmartre and elsewhere, songwriters are launching satirical couplets in which I'm rather denigrated. Thanks to you, that's going to stop."

"Let's not sell the bearskin," cautioned the great bloodhound.

"Ah! I'm confident with you on the case," Lereni assured him, "I would bet anyone that in eight days time you'll have unmasked the Ladykiller."

His forehead suddenly blushing, the official detective observed, "However, I wonder if I can accept your very generous and selfless offer…"

"What's stopping you?" exclaimed Météor's boss.

"I'll confess, my dear master, that the more I think about it, the more vexed I am to realise I'll garner laurel wreaths I've not earned, and receive congratulations from all sides when I ought to receive only accusations."

"Those scruples do you credit," replied the noble bloodhound, "and they don't astonish me, coming from you. Meanwhile, you're going to do me the honour of putting them to one side."

"However…"

"There's no however about it. I've told you my conditions; I'll add only one word, that I cleave perhaps more to the second than to the first."

Chantecoq stood and approached his old comrade, and said to him with that charming bonhomie with which he knew how to win over all those he wanted to conquer.

"Come now! My dear, you're too up to date with things and theatrical people not to know that it frequently happens that plays written in collaboration bear only one author's name…"

"Certainly, my dear master," retorted Lereni. "But permit me to respectfully observe, the author who has not signed it receives a somewhat higher portion of the credit than his colleague."

Chantecoq asked, "Do you imagine that if I should triumph, the pleasure I will first feel at having put an end to this dreadful massacre, and then of supporting you, wouldn't be worth more than anything?"

And with an expression of very cordial and very emotional abandon, the king of detectives continued. "My friend, I'm under no illusions. I'll soon reach the autumn of my career. Not that I aspire to rest. The man who still feels strong enough to take care of himself has no right to abandon action, any more than a general, after winning several victories, can declare without betrayal, 'I've won enough battles. I've won the right to taste the leisures and joys of peacetime.'

131

"Cincinnatus[10] will return to his plough only when Rome has no more enemies to vanquish. In our age, all men who still feel in their prime have no right to renounce action. So long as I don't experience any mental or physical deterioration, I'll remain on watch and I'll continue, even solely through love of humanity, to defend society against criminals who, every day - we must, alas, acknowledge that - inflict their ever more terrible blows upon it.

"That's why, my dear friend, in admitting that I'm obliging you, helping you get hold of the Ladykiller, I consider that you're doing me a far greater service in allowing me to realise my dearest wish, a wish which can be summarised in one single word: service!"

Overcome by this argument which, in raising the stakes, no longer permitted Lereni a moment's hesitation, the commissioner cried, "My dear master, I can only bow before your will."

"Just in time!"

"Give me your directives, your orders, I'll obey you."

Chantecoq replied, "For this evening, I have only one piece of information to ask of you. I'll summarise it with this brief question: *today*, how many victims has the Ladykiller claimed?"

"None," replied the chief of police.

"You're absolutely sure of that?"

---

[10] Lucius Quinctius Cincinnatus (c.519 BC - c.430 BC). A legendary figure of the Roman Republic, Cincinnatus was a Roman patrician who was twice appointed dictator (in the strictest sense of the word) to defend Rome against invasion, and twice relinquished his powers only to return to his small farm. Many details of his life are disputed.

"Absolutely. This evening, before coming to see you, I returned to my office and no case had been reported."

"Perfect."

Lereni observed, "It could very well be that the wretch, having noticed you were taking an interest in him, renounced his series of crimes."

Chantecoq thought for a moment. Then he shook his head.

"I don't believe so," he said. "I'm convinced it's only an interruption, and that this interruption is due only to a physical obstacle."

And Chantecoq added, "Therefore, phone headquarters; I would be unduly surprised if you were informed that, since your departure, there has been news that the Ladykiller has perpetrated one or even several new attacks."

At once, Lereni grabbed the phone and asked for the number he needed. He didn't have much trouble getting a connection and at once asked for the duty commander, who made haste to run to the phone.

"Hello! It's me, the chief," said the policeman. "Is that you, Vernin?"

"Yes, chief."

"What news?"

"We had reports of two new Ladykiller killings, one on Avenue Champs-Elysées, at the Grand Palais, and the other on Avenue de la Grande-Armée, on street level, outside number 52."

"Could the victims be identified?"

"Yes, one is the wife of a senior civil servant in the Treasury, and the other is the wife of the president of a large insurance company."

"At what time were these crimes committed?"

"The first at eight o'clock in the evening, and the second at nine o'clock."

"Thank you," said Monsieur Lereni, hanging up the receiver.

Turning to Chantecoq, he said, "You were right. The Ladykiller has returned, as you could tell from the questions I asked my colleague."

"I was certain of it," declared Chantecoq, who seemed modestly triumphant.

And he continued. "I can't tell you anything further as yet. You once worked under my direction and you have certainly not forgotten that I don't much like to make predictions and that I communicate the hypotheses I can conceive only when they have become concrete for me.

"All I can tell you is that the news you've just given me, though disastrous for the two poor women who died, is excellent for my investigation; because it permits me to establish a very useful overlap, whose effects you will soon observe."

"I'm delighted with what you're telling me," replied the chief of police. "As you recommended, I'll return at once to my office and give instructions to my subordinate."

With a gesture, Chantecoq stopped his colleague and said in a strange tone, under which a certain mischief could be detected, "Are you still single?"

Lereni replied, "If I had married, my dear master, be assured you would have been the first to know."

With a more and more mischievous air, Chantecoq continued. "No important appointments?"

"None."

"The night is yours?"

134

"The night is mine."

"Then," said the great bloodhound, "we can do some useful work."

And he pressed an electric buzzer. A man stood before him: it was Météor, who had just rushed into the room.

The king of detectives was not a man for great introductions. At once, he said, "My dear Lereni, meet my secretary and collaborator, Météor. I won't sing his praises to you in his presence. Let me tell you simply that it will soon be three years since I employed him. That's worth more, I believe, than anything."

Monsieur Lereni offered his hand cordially to Météor, who, obeying his boss's orders, had taken down from beginning to end the conversation the great bloodhound had just had with the chief of police.

Chantecoq replied at once. "Now, Météor, we're going to collaborate secretly with the police. I don't need to recommend you keep silent on this. I know, better than anyone, how respectful you are of professional secrecy."

Météor felt he needed to trump this. "Boss, I would sooner bite off my tongue and swallow it like beef steak, rather than…"

Chantecoq interrupted him. "We're not here to create literature, still less to do any cooking. So be quiet and don't be daft."

Météor put a finger on his lips, which indicated he had decided not to utter a single syllable more, until such time as he had his master's permission.

That master continued, "Put on outfit number 27; come back and meet me here and I'll tell you then what you have to do."

Météor gave a simple nod of agreement and evaporated

with the same speed with which he had appeared.

Lereni replied. "That lad seems very intelligent to me."

"And so he is," confirmed the king of detectives. "I'm more and more satisfied, because he doesn't content himself with being of useful day to day service to me. He's shown a devotion and affection towards me which have made me rather fond of him. Sure, he still has much to learn. But I'm convinced that in a few years, he'll be highly capable of setting up his own agency in turn and revealing himself as a first rate detective.

"He's in the process of camouflaging himself, my dear Lereni, because despite all the theories of modern policing, I've not given up on a system which once obtained such great success and which still does for me these days."

"I acknowledge that there's some good in it and even some excellence," declared Monsieur Lereni. "The trick lies in knowing how to make use of it and, unless you're extremely crafty in the art of giving oneself a makeover, it very often happens that an agent's disguise goes awry and they make themselves more easily recognisable by those they are trying to pursue than if they had given chase under their true appearance."

"You're absolutely right, my dear," replied the great bloodhound. "The truth, you see, is that one must never be absolute in anything. All systems have some good, all have some bad; because - alas! - the older I get, the more I realise that perfection is not of this world.

"The essential thing is to take, leave, and be inspired by all the character traits of the people with whom one has dealings and from the circumstances in which the mysteries that one has to unravel are presented.

"As such, in the case at hand, I'm having my secretary

136

camouflage himself. And me, this evening, I'm going to present my natural appearance, and you, well, let's see… no, there's nothing to fear! You can come with me; I'm bringing you, without sparking the slightest suspicion, to the home of the game that we are hunting."

"May I ask you, my dear master, what role you have in mind for me in the play on which we are going to collaborate?"

"Oh! A very important role, be sure of that, and one which will soon become, I believe, the lead."

The chief of police didn't press him. Knowing Chantecoq like the back of his hand, he knew that the man detested questions and didn't like sharing his intentions, even to his closest allies.

As he had done on several occasions; when, once, he had served under his command, he said to himself, "I only have to trail after him, and to follow him where he leads me."

Chantecoq, guessing all that was going on in his friend's mind, asked, "Are you armed?"

"Well enough to defend myself," replied the policeman.

"I shall do likewise," replied Chantecoq. "But the kind of weapon I use in such cases certainly doesn't resemble yours."

Chantecoq headed towards his safe, activated its secret mechanism and, having opened it, plunged his right hand inside, pulling out two metal boxes of around thirty square centimetres. With a wilfully mysterious attitude, he said simply,

"One contains life and the other locks away death.

"But that's not all," he continued. "The methods you will perhaps have the opportunity to see me use are insufficient to defend us against the Ladykiller, because while admitting that we may be spotted by him, he can very well employ

137

procedures of which he's made use on those that he wanted to make vanish and to send us, my secretary, you, and myself, into eternity, without us even having time to bid a final farewell to our friends and acquaintances.

"So, I believe we might be well advised, from this moment on, to take measures to avoid such an awfully big adventure, whose consequences would be more than disastrous, but irreparable."

Lereni replied, smiling, "I'm sure you've already found the way to relieve this danger."

"Oh! Ages ago," retorted Chantecoq. "This even dates back to 1917. While I was hunting spies, imagine I had discovered that one of our enemies, who succeeded in infiltrating French territory and who was none other than one of the most reputed scholars of one of the countries with whom we were at war, had invented an injection system thanks to which he could instantly kill all the people bothering him.

"Thanks to the admirable intelligence services which were operating on our side, we spotted this scoundrel before he could begin the series of his sinister exploits. There's no need to tell you he was aiming very high indeed; I have no need to explain further. Luckily indeed, the individuals whom he had resolved to assassinate were extremely well guarded and it was not easy for him to approach them.

"Despite everything, in such cases, a surprise is always to be feared, and this is what I imagined in order to rid us of this serpent's fatal bite: I went to a chemist attached to the Ministry of War who had already rendered great services for his country, as much for his genius discoveries as for his skillful and prompt fashion of exploiting them usefully.[11]

"I made him aware of the situation and I asked him, a little naively, no doubt, if he didn't know of some product or if he couldn't make one which could immunise people against this spy's jabs.

"While I was talking to him, this gentle and great scholar watched me with a slightly mocking attitude, so I believed at first that he took me for a madman and was going to politely show me the door.

"I was mistaken. Indeed, when I had finished my explanation, very amiably, my chemist replied to me, in the most natural tones, 'Nothing simpler. I already developed, well before the War, a product which shields against insect and snake bites; I managed an excellent result, of which many of our explorers and colonial forces have made successful use. The tiresome thing is that the effect of this product lasts only twenty-four hours. Then it's necessary to take a very hot bath and to rebrush the whole body with my pommade which, however, dries instantly and provokes no irritation of the skin. And by modifying my formula oh so slightly, I'm completely certain it could be used very effectively to protect against this scoundrel's imminent attacks.'

"'My dear master,' I responded, 'never mind that. Entrust your formula to me, whose secret I swear to you I will respect, and I guarantee you that within forty-eight hours this will all be finished and I will have crushed the viper.'

"This good scholar, to whom I was recommended by a letter signed by the Interior Minister, said to me, 'Come back to see me tomorrow morning and I'll give you the formula in

---

[11] It seems likely that this is Jean Aubry, from *Chantecoq and the Aubry Affair*, and *Chantecoq and Wilhelm's Spy*.

question.' Which is what he did.

"As he gave me the paper on which he had written the old formula, he said, 'You can be completely reassured; I've just tested it on myself, injecting myself with a dose of poison capable of taking down a cow. You can see that I'm as healthy as yesterday. You can therefore, Monsieur Chantecoq, be completely confident.'

"I left, after having thanked the scholar who, through the simple instinct of his genius, was going to save the life of all those of whom France had such great need.

"I went to a chemist whose address he had given me and who had prepared his formula and, that same evening, I was taking home enough to anoint my body abundantly. I must acknowledge that this pommade didn't have the inconveniences of so many others; it's not sticky, or foul-smelling; and, as soon as it touches your skin, it blends in with it so well, that after a few seconds one has the impression that it's evaporated completely.

"The following morning, I brushed my whole body with this product. Full of confidence in my chemist's claims - and subsequent events were to prove how right I was - I set out on the trail of the spy, on whom I had, anyway, a complete report, and on whom I already possessed some information which put me on his trail.

"But I was dealing with a crafty operator. The pursuit looked to be long and laborious. So I resolved to cut things short. Instead of disguising myself, I presented myself under my natural appearance in the comfortable room he was occupying in an excellent house on the left bank. He recognised me at once. I had already had dealings with him, but that's another story which would take too long to recount. He flushed slightly, then he recovered his composure at once.

"Not yet having my famous tranquiliser pistol at my disposal, which allows me to put my adversaries to sleep at a stroke and which has rendered me and will render me still so many services, I drew my Browning brusquely and I said, 'You're *done*. There's no point resisting me.'

"My spy immediately put his hands in the air. I approached, to put the handcuffs on him. But he had some skill and agility. With a single punch, he sent my gun flying across the room.

"Then, grabbing me by the arm, he put me in a grip from which it would have been easy for me to escape. But I wanted to see the experiment through to the end, to catch him in the act, so as to be certain he was indeed the man I was seeking.

"So, just for form's sake, I pretended to struggle. But after a few wilfully weak efforts, I began to cry, 'Let me go… you're hurting me… you're breaking my bones… Enough! Come on! Enough!'

"He burst into sardonic laughter. And, while he was continuing to paralyse my arm with a ju-jitsu hold, whose effect it would have been easy to counter, he took from a nearby table a very sharp needle that he pushed slowly into my skin. That was what I was waiting for!

"I immediately bent my legs. He released his hold and I fell to the floor. I then heard him murmur in French, 'Now I'll have to get rid of this carcass! But that's not going to be so very difficult.'

"He leaned over me. I surged up like a leaping tiger. Because, at that time, I was in my prime."

"You still are," Lereni observed in passing.

Chantecoq finished. "I gave my assassin a formidable

hook to the jaw, which knocked him out instantly. But I'm abridging. Six weeks later, the rogue was shot by firing squad at the Vincennes barracks. Excuse this lengthy tale."

"It was extremely interesting," Lereni assured him.

"In any case," continued the famous bloodhound, "it proves we must be completely confident in our chemist's formula. That's why, before setting off into battle, I invite you to do like me, to coat your body with this precious unguent which will make us, for at least twenty-four hours, safe against any attack. I ordered a sufficient quantity to permit us to face victoriously the monster that we want to take down, should you accept."

"I accept."

"Please follow me to my bathroom, then."

"My dear master," declared the chief of police, who was finding great peace in this collaboration with Chantecoq, as it calmed his keen anxieties, "my dear master, if you weren't the very model of disinterest, you could make an immense fortune at this point in time."

"How so?" the king of detectives asked.

"You'd only have to put a note in the papers announcing you had found a way to protect unfaithful spouses from the Ladykiller's fatal sting. Twenty-four hours later, you would have more than enough orders."

"That's likely indeed," cried Chantecoq. "But that's an operation I mustn't even think of. First, the formula doesn't belong to me and I don't have any right to use it for anything but personal use. Then, I find it simpler to attack evil at its root rather than use an empirical method which would have every appearance of a quack's remedy."

And in a mysterious but energetically affirmative tone, the king of detectives said, "In any case, it's only a matter of time

142

and even of very little time. And you'll see, my dear Lereni, we won't need to use that kind of advertising to save those unfortunate people from the Ladykiller's deadly stings."

10 WHERE THE MYSTERY, RATHER THAN BEING SOLVED, SEEMS INSTEAD TO BE FURTHER COMPLICATED

What Chantecoq, always so prudent in his declarations and even so miserly with his words, had not wanted to say, even to the chief of police, we will now reveal to our readers.

It's indispensable, for the clarity of that which follows, that all those who do us the honour of taking an interest in this tale should be, from this point, up to date with everything that was going on within the mind of the king of detectives.

He was no longer in doubt. For him, the culprit could be none other than Professor Courtil. And here is how he came to this conclusion.

Monsieur Lereni, by confirming to him that, from the morning until eight in the evening, the Ladykiller had not committed any murders, drew his attention to the fact that this pause in the crime spree corresponded exactly with the time he spent in Professor Courtil's company.

What substantiated this opinion, was that the attacks had

resumed almost immediately after he had taken leave of the scholar.

Moreover, recalling the information that Météor had brought him concerning the strange chemist of Rue Bonaparte, he had followed this line of thought:

"Courtil was betrayed by his wife, whom he adored, and made her disappear, by poisoning her.

"Having nothing to fear from justice, he either made her swallow a toxin which left only minute traces in her system, some lesions that could be attributed to natural causes. As his personal situation put him above all suspicion, he could, in all security, accomplish what he would consider to be an act of justice.

"But soon, tormented by remorse, he tried to forget the past through isolation, in solitude, when he voluntarily exiled himself to the tiny Breton villa in Rospoden where, to keep busy, he gave himself over to studies in his laboratory towards which his genius was pushing him. And it was at that moment he discovered the procedure which consists of restoring to life those who, while having every appearance of death, are nonetheless only plunged into lethargy or catalepsy.

"But little by little, despite the powerful diversions to which he had recourse, to save his mind from the terrible memory which haunted him, he gradually came to lose if not all his reason, but at the very least a large part of his self-control.

"A fixed idea lodged in his brain: becoming the implacable vigilante against adulterous women.

"Soon turning to monomania, this idea turned a man who could have been one of humanity's most illustrious benefactors, into a dangerous madman, who doesn't deserve

145

justice, but a mental institution…

"When he discovered the formula for his lethal injection, he returned to Paris. Why didn't he make use of it at once? Why did he wait several years to begin his series of sinister exploits?

"He alone can tell us. In any case, what's most important, is first to stop him in his dealing of death and then to get hold of him and see if it's a matter for the courts, or the shed."

As Chantecoq was finishing those words, a young agent in uniform, his upper lip adorned with an American-style moustache, entered the study without being announced.

On seeing him, the chief of police couldn't help a start of surprise. At once, the king of detectives explained this apparition which was as sudden as it was unexpected, saying,

"This is our good friend Météor, who I ordered to put on this costume, thanks to which he'll be able, very soon, to keep watch while we are in action."

And he added, "My dear Lereni, I'll take you to my bathroom, so you may coat yourself with the unguent of which I just spoke."

"Understood," agreed the senior civil servant, whose trust in Chantecoq was such that he would have gladly followed him to the ends of the earth.

So, both of them left the study. But in the doorway, the great bloodhound turned back and said to his secretary, "While you're waiting for us, go and stroll up and down in front of 37 Rue Bonaparte, where we'll join you in around an hour; take a taxi and go quickly, because I don't know if you might not have the opportunity to glean something interesting."

"Understood boss," Météor obeyed at once.

While watching the private detective and the policeman vanish, he muttered to himself, "The sacred union, it's a fine thing all the same!"

***

At ten o'clock in the evening, Chantecoq and Monsieur Lereni rang at Professor Courtil's door.

At first, no one answered.

Chantecoq said in his companion's ear, "They've not yet gone to bed, because I saw a light and Météor just told us he noticed, not ten minutes ago, the professor's silhouette behind the curtains of his window.

"We just need to ring a bit louder, because Madame Scholastic, as I've already observed, has a somewhat lazy ear, and the professor's bedroom must be at the other end of the apartment."

Chantecoq began to ring insistently. But the door still wouldn't open. Lereni observed, "Perhaps we've been spotted and they don't want to open the door to us?"

"That would astonish me," said the great bloodhound. "There must be other reasons than that."

At the same moment, a strident whistle came from the street, repeated three times in a row.

Chantecoq said at once, "That's a signal from Météor. It means something very important is going on below. Let's go down quickly."

They both descended the staircase. After having burst through the building's door, they found themselves facing Météor, who said to them at once with vivacity, "You'd hardly gone up to Professor Courtil's apartment when I saw a man with a white beard, completely matching the

147

Ladykiller's description, come out of the house and get into a chauffeur-driven car, a very plain vehicle which was waiting a few numbers up the road.

"I couldn't see if there was anyone else in the car, but, in any case, I was able to take its number and here it is: 31.27-RB-6."

"Good," Chantecoq said. "Which way did it go?"

"Towards Boulevard Saint-Germain."

"Which leads me to think," said Chantecoq, as though he was talking to himself, "that our man is going to be operating tonight on the left bank, probably on the Montparnasse side, so long as it's not in some ministry or ambassadorial residence where there might be a party."

"Indeed," Lereni interrupted, "tonight there's a grand reception at the Ministry of Commerce."

"Aha!" emphasised the great bloodhound, "It would perhaps be interesting to go and take a look at that. Unfortunately, we're not dressed for it. We won't be able to get into the rooms and see if the man with the white beard can be found there."

"It's also possible," mused the chief of police, "that he's operating at the guests' exit."

"That hardly seems likely to me," replied Chantecoq. "For some time now, the alarm has been given. He must be staying on his guard and acting with a certain prudence.

"So, I believe it would be better, all things considered, to quietly await his return here, and snap him up in passing."

"I'm completely of your opinion," agreed Lereni.

"And yet, I believe we would do better not to give the appearance of waiting for him," declared Chantecoq. "So we'll walk up and down, leaving to our friend Météor the

148

duty of attracting our attention to this man with a white beard, as soon as he reappears."

"I believe, indeed, that this is the wisest course of action," agreed the chief of police.

While Météor continued to keep watch, Chantecoq and Lereni began to wander along the pavement.

"Oh, my dear," said the former to the latter, "why do you seem so preoccupied?"

"I wonder if that man with the white beard really is Professor Courtil, or one of his accomplices."

"Upon what do you base this hesitation?"

"Upon the fact that your secretary noticed very shortly before our arrival the professor's silhouette behind his curtains; which would seem *a priori* to indicate it was not he who, just now, got into that taxi."

"Why?"

"If he was, we would certainly have met him when we were going up to him…"

"The house could have a service staircase," Chantecoq objected judiciously.

"In any case," declared the chief of police, "he would have had to disguise himself very quickly."

"You know," replied the king of detectives, "it doesn't take long to stick on a wig and glue a beard to your chin, especially when you're used to it."

"That's true. Anyway, I'm of the opinion that, even if we must stay here for several hours, we mustn't abandon our post."

"I was just going to say that," declared Chantecoq.

"Are you still good at piquet?"[12]

149

"I play from time to time," replied Chantecoq, "and I believe I've not forgotten too much."

"It's a shame there's no cafe nearby. We could use our time profitably."

Chantecoq replied, smiling, "I couldn't ask better than to be beaten, or even to beat you, but my flair tells me we might not be waiting long for the return of the man with the white beard. It's already nearly eleven o'clock and, from the research I've done, the Ladykiller never murders after midnight."

"Then let's await his return," cried the chief of police.

And with an accent of melancholy gravity, he added, "To think that at this moment the wretch could well be fatally injecting some new victims and we're both powerless to disarm him."

Chantecoq observed, "I have indeed thought of asking you to telephone police headquarters, to send some officers with all haste to the Ministry of Commerce, giving them the description of the individual in question; but I at once reflected that it was perhaps a waste of time and that they would arrive too late. If there's a crime, it must be in the process of being committed."

"I had the same thought as you," declared Lereni, "and I must say I quickly arrived at the same conclusion. Nothing to do but await events, or rather our fellow."

Around half an hour passed. The two friends had not ceased strolling in the street and had ended up exchanging words which no longer had any connection to the case in which they had joined forces by common accord. Suddenly, as they were approaching number 37, Météor rushed towards

---

[12] Piquet is an old two player card game played with a 32 card deck.

them and said,

"There's the car coming back; I recognise it, that's the one, I'm sure."

A saloon car was coasting to a halt a few numbers before arriving at the building occupied by Professor Courtil.

Someone stepped down from it. It was not the man with the white beard, but a clean-shaven character, dressed not in a redingote and black bowler hat, but wearing a suit jacket and a grey felt hat with a black ribbon.

As he was approaching number 37, Chantecoq, whom he had not noticed, as well as his companions, who were also hiding in the crevice of a porte cochere, recognised Professor Courtil immediately.

In a low voice, he said to the chief of police, "Don't move. Let me handle this."

Crossing the path, he joined the scholar, just as he was pulling on the bellrope.

"Good evening, my dear professor," he said in a deliberately friendly voice.

Courtil gave a slight start; then, turning back, he said, recognising the great bloodhound, "Hold on, is that you, Monsieur Chantecoq? Is this a chance meeting or were you coming to see me?"

"I was coming to see you," said the king of detectives, weighing each word carefully. "There have been developments of which you must be unaware, and I've come to tell you about them."

"What then?"

"The Ladykiller has resumed his exploits."

Professor Courtil replied in the most natural tone. "That was to be expected."

The concierge having decided to pull the rope, the

building's door opened, and Professor Courtil held out his hand to Chantecoq, demonstrating his clear intention to take leave of him.

But the king of detectives insisted: "I would like to have a chat about this matter, Professor."

"This evening? It's very late," the scholar said evasively.

"Tomorrow," replied the bloodhound, "it will perhaps be *too late*."

Without the slightest awkwardness, Courtil replied, meeting his visitor's gaze, "So it's an immediate interview you would like to have with me, then?"

"Yes, monsieur, if, at any rate, I'm not abusing your hospitality."

Courtil replied, "No, you're not abusing anything. Although I'm used to going to bed no later than midnight, I'm disposed to make an exception for you."

"I am infinitely grateful," declared Chantecoq.

And in a tone which had again become friendly, the scholar answered, "Do follow me, please."

The king of detectives didn't hesitate for a moment to follow at the professor's heels. He switched on the light on the staircase, which they both climbed without speaking a word. They reached the landing on the second floor.

Monsieur Courtil put a key in his door's lock, which he opened and closed again, after letting Chantecoq pass ahead of him.

At once, he switched on the lights and led the king of detectives straight into his office.

With great courtesy, he indicated to him a seat on which Chantecoq sat down, and he perched on an armchair, before his table which was encumbered with paperwork and books.

"Monsieur Chantecoq," said the professor, "I'm

listening."

The great bloodhound was well aware of the importance of the game he was about to play.

It consisted, indeed, for him, either in wringing a confession from he who he believed to be guilty, or provoking him into some act which would be equivalent to a confession.

Never yet had an accused party been subjected to an interrogation that was more crafty, or tight.

Chantecoq began. "Professor, here is, in a few words, the purpose of my visit. Perhaps you're unaware, but I've come to inform you: the Ladykiller has claimed some new victims…"

"As I said just now, I was completely unaware of that," declared Courtil with an imperturbable air and a tone whose good faith could not be doubted.

"Ah well! Here it is," continued the king of detectives. "This evening, at eight o'clock, the wife of a senior civil servant in the Treasury and that of the president of the board of a large insurance company have been murdered: one at eight o'clock, on the Avenue Champs-Elysées. The other at nine o'clock, on Avenue de la Grande-Armée."

"Oh! Really," intoned the scholar.

"But that's not all."

And while staring into the eyes of the professor, who held his gaze with disarming candour, the king of detectives rapped out, "That's not all: barely half an hour ago, at a reception held by the Ministry of Commerce, the Ladykiller struck again."

This time, Courtil could not hold back a slight shiver.

"How do you know already?" he asked, expressing sharp astonishment.

Chantecoq wasn't the kind of man to be caught out. He possessed, however, to the supreme degree, the art of eluding embarrassing questions.

"You don't believe me?" he shouted.

And before the professor had time to protest, he took hold of the telephone and said in a peremptory tone, "Give me the Ministry for Commerce at once... urgent business..."

Chantecoq certainly had to exercise on the telephone personnel an irresistible influence and due to a special fluid, whose secret he will hopefully perhaps one day give us, to calm our nerves, he obtained the connection almost immediately.

At once, he spoke into the receiver, in his ringing voice, "It's Jacques Bellegarde here, editor of the *Petit Parisien*. Please give me the Minister at once or, in his place, one of his deputies."

While he was waiting for his connection, Chantecoq glanced towards the professor.

He, very calm, at least in appearance, hardly seemed to be paying any attention to what was about to be said. He was looking at the ceiling with a weary air and repressing successive yawns, which demonstrated he had an urgent need for sleep and was waiting, not without a certain amount of impatience, for the moment when he could go to bed.

A voice rang out on the other end of the line. "Is that you, Monsieur Bellegarde?"

"Yes, indeed."

"Monsieur Deltaillé here, chief secretary to the office of the Minister for Commerce."

"Very well, monsieur. Forgive me for disturbing you."

"Only too happy, Monsieur Bellegarde, if I can be of service to you."

"Thank you. Is it correct that the Ladykiller committed, during the Minister's reception, a new crime?"

"Two!"

"Oh! Really!" exclaimed the king of detectives, passing the second receiver to Monsieur Courtil who, with a nonchalant hand, pressed his ear to it.

The deputy continued.

"It wasn't just one victim that the wretch struck, but two, and two charming ladies: Madame Belmont, the publisher of the literary revue: *L'art de la pensée*, and the wife of Doctor Desruelles, who had just been named as a fellow of the Faculty of Medicine."

The civil servant spoke nervously. "We are wondering how this wretch could have got in…"

But, brusquely, the line went dead. Chantecoq did not ask for it to be restored. For the moment, at least, he didn't need to ask any more. His flair had not misled him. Now, he was entirely convinced of it: he had the Ladykiller in front of him.

The final battle was about to begin.

"You see, my dear master," said the bloodhound to the professor, "I was not mistaken."

"You have, indeed, a prodigious gift of intuition," declared the scholar.

Slowly, Chantecoq articulated, "I was informed, too late unfortunately to prevent these two new crimes, but sufficiently to be certain of many things."

"Do you know who the culprit could be?" asked Courtil, without the slightest obvious emotion.

"Oh yes, I know him," said Chantecoq.

And in a strange voice, he added, "I believe you know him much better than I do."

155

"I don't understand," said the professor, without straying for a moment from his calm.

"Let's say rather," replied the bloodhound, "you don't want to understand."

Suddenly, Professor Courtil stood up. And, while a flame, which could have been provoked as much by indignation as by rage, lit in his eyes, he intoned, "Ah! Monsieur Chantecoq, would you do me the injustice ~~and~~ of suspecting me?"

Anyone other than the king of detectives would not have failed to be deeply impressed by this virulent outburst and would certainly have lost for a moment and, perhaps even completely, the composure that the circumstances required.

But the great bloodhound was of that breed who knew to remain always absolutely in control of themselves. And, without revealing any trace of what was going on inside his head, he contented himself with saying, "No, my dear master, *I don't suspect you!*"

In responding in this way, Chantecoq was not lying. Indeed, he didn't *suspect* the scholar, as he was *convinced* he was indeed the Ladykiller.

All the cross checking he had just done could leave no doubt remaining in him.

The truth, he possessed it entirely.

Courtil disposed of his wife, because she betrayed him. That dreadful episode managed to disturb his rationality, already tested so sorely by the odious ostracism, the abominable quarantine which he was forced to suffer by his colleagues.

Gradually, he let a fixed idea invade his brain: that of becoming a sort of mysterious vigilante who charged themselves with inflicting on unfaithful women the dreadful punishment that, in his view, they deserved.

He had taken years to carry out his project, either because, despite his genius, he hadn't found the formula he needed for his executions, or because he encountered, very plausibly, difficulties in establishing a secret information service which permitted him to strike with certainty.

In any case, Chantecoq was convinced: the assassin, or rather the madman, was indeed the man who had just stood up before him.

The light in his eyes, the rictus of his mouth, the clenching of his fists, the pallor of his skin, and even the hoarseness of his voice could only reinforce him in his opinion.

But he still lacked the physical evidence, which he needed to bring this man to justice.

This evidence, he could obtain only through confessions or through the discovery of incriminating items or accusing documents.

Understanding he would obtain nothing by violence, he told himself that, to winkle his secret from him, he would need to press into service all the resources of his skill and experience.

The professor, visibly reassured by Chantecoq's careful answer, replied in a tone which revealed a certain degree of anxiety, "Monsieur detective, as you don't suspect me, why did you claim, only a moment ago, that I knew the Ladykiller as well as and even better than you?"

This question was so direct, so dangerous, and it proved that beyond his fixation the professor had conserved his lucidity, but it didn't appear to vex the famous policeman at all.

"My dear master," he replied, "this evening, around ten o'clock, I came to ring at your door. No one answered."

With a certain eagerness, Courtil stressed, "Nothing surprising about that, dear monsieur. My servant was already in bed, and sleep has the result of exacerbating her already considerable deafness. As to me, I had gone out."

Delicately, the bloodhound probed. "Are you quite sure of that, my dear master?"

"Why yes, of course," replied the scholar, who the king of detectives was leading, step by step, unknowingly, into exchanging fire with him.

And with the most deferential politeness, he continued. "I believe you're making a small error."

With a certain nervousness, the professor exclaimed, "I rather believe it's you who are mistaken!"

"No, my dear master," the king of detectives insisted courteously. "After returning to the street, I instinctively raised my eyes to your windows, and, behind one of them, I definitely recognised your silhouette. I even had the very clear impression that you were in the process of putting on a wig and gluing a fake beard to your chin."

"Me?" cried the scholar, "A fake beard, a wig? Why, damnit, do you think I would dress myself up in hairpieces? I fear, Monsieur Chantecoq, that your detective's imagination may have dragged you a bit too far."

"That's possible, in the end," the skilled bloodhound pretended to concede. "But then, I would be grateful if you could shed light on certain points which remain rather obscure to my mind."

"What are they?" Courtil exclaimed, not noticing that he was engaging more and more in a contest of arms in which he risked getting caught out at any moment.

"Let's proceed with order and method," declared Chantecoq, who now felt he was dominating his host more and more. "I must begin by telling you that, from the moment I came down from your apartment, after having rung in vain at your door, the entrance to your building did not cease for a single moment to be the object of careful surveillance, and I have thus acquired the certain knowledge that other than an old man with a white beard, no one crossed its threshold. There are two things from that: either you stayed at home, or you went out in disguise. Now, you didn't stay at home, because I saw you return. Therefore, you're the man in the white beard."

Cornered by this magisterial reasoning, Courtil, nevertheless, defended himself. "Who's to say, Monsieur Chantecoq, that there is no other way out of this house? I could very well have taken that exit to go out."

"Then why didn't you take it again to re-enter?"

"I don't have to explain my actions to anyone."

"That's an argument I've often heard used by people who, such as yourself, have a powerful interest in hiding the details of their existence."

"Monsieur Chantecoq, I must warn you that you're beginning to wear out my patience."

"Why?"

"You're trying to dupe me."

"Me?"

"Yes, you!"

"How so?"

"Just now, you affirmed to me that you didn't suspect me of being the Ladykiller."

"I'm prepared to repeat that affirmation."

"So…?"

"I'll add simply that I'm *sure* you're the man in the white beard."

"And when would that be?"

"And when would that be?" repeated Chantecoq with a smile of acute irony. "When would that be? That would prove in the clearest, most blatant, most inarguable fashion, that I was right not to *suspect*, but *to be sure* that you are the murderer of all those unfortunate…"

A terrible gleam sparked in the eyes of the hunted man that was the scholar. And in a voice trembling with menace and not fear, he said,

"Take care, Monsieur Chantecoq, take care!"

"Of what?"

"At this moment, you're at my mercy."

"I rather believe it's you who are at mine."

"We shall see…"

And the king of detectives who, a few seconds beforehand had seen Courtil plunge his hand into one of the half-open drawers of his table, reached out towards him as though he wanted to grab him by the collar.

But with terrifying speed, Courtil grabbed his wrist and stabbed it with a needle that, surreptitiously, he had taken from the drawer.

Chantecoq collapsed heavily on the floor. Immobile, his mouth half-opened, his eyes staring, nostrils flaring, the scholar contemplated his fresh victim, who seemed to have been instantly struck down by the toxin that he had just injected into him.

Then he darted to the back of his office, and opened a door which led inside a black cabinet which had no other opening.

He came back towards Chantecoq, who was maintaining a corpse-like rigidity, and grabbing him by the ankles, he tried to drag him over to the cabinet. But he didn't get far.

Indeed, reviving suddenly and springing to his feet like a jack springing from a box, the king of detectives half knocked out his adversary with a fearsome left hook to the jaw and, grabbing him by the arm to prevent him from falling, he carried him into the black doorless cabinet and locked him in there, taking care to leave the key in the lock.

This task accomplished in less time than it took to describe it, Chantecoq rushed towards the window, which looked out over the street, and opened it wide.

Then, leaning outside, he let out a resounding "Hey!", which made Monsieur Lereni and Météor raise their heads.

Those two, conforming to the master's instructions, had continued to maintain a vigilant watch on the professor's house.

With a gesture, the skillful bloodhound invited them to join him, which they did at once.

Chantecoq opened the door and welcomed them with these words, "It's done: I have the proof it was him and I've got him. Follow me."

The king of detectives led them to the room where the scene we described just unfolded.

"He's in there," said the private policeman, pointing out the black cabinet to them.

And he added, "I knocked him out, but it's best we take precautions."

He armed himself with a Browning from his jacket pocket and, approaching the cabinet door, he pressed his ear against the panel.

No noise could be heard.

"He must not have woken up yet," murmured Chantecoq.

Nevertheless, with the prudence that characterised him,

he turned the key in the lock quietly. As the door was grinding on its hinges, the bloodhound gave a cry of rage! The opening was empty: Professor Courtil had vanished!

11 THE MAN HUNT

The king of detectives, who was containing only with great difficulty the internal rage with which he was shaking, cried out, his brows furrowed,

"It seems this bandit is much less crazy than I supposed."

He fell silent, because it wasn't the moment to speak, or to reason, but to act.

Signalling his two companions to keep quiet, he entered the cabinet and began to tap the walls with the butt of his revolver.

Then, turning back to Monsieur Lereni and Météor, he said to them, "It's certain that this cabinet possesses a secret exit which must lead to a neighbouring apartment that Courtil must have rented under a false name, unless it was arranged by acquaintances... no, this isn't the time to find out how the Ladykiller was able to flee, but to do our best to pick up his trail.

"I'm going to wake old Scholastic, who is sleeping in the apartment, and do my best to glean some information from her. Météor, you stay here. My dear Lereni, please accompany me."

The servant's bedroom was situated at the other end of the apartment.

Chantecoq and his friend didn't have a great deal of trouble finding it.

Indeed, on entering the waiting room of which we already know, they heard loud and prolonged snoring, which immediately guided them towards Scholastic's bedroom.

They noticed the door was not locked and entered the room without any difficulty at all.

The brave woman was sleeping, as always, like a log. Several times, Chantecoq coughed. Lereni imitated him, but she didn't budge.

They started to move furniture, even dropping a chair. Successive noises produced no results.

Chantecoq decided to take the sleeper by her arm and shake her, gently at first, then with growing energy.

Poor Scholastic finally let out a vague groan of protest; then she tried to turn back against the wall. But she didn't manage it.

The king of detectives seized her with his iron grip. The servant let out a cry of pain.

"Is that you, Professor? Oh! Let me go, you're hurting me!"

Chantecoq loosened his grip a little. Then he heard Scholastic murmur. "There he is again having his fit. When he's like that, I'm always afraid he'll hurt me."

"Don't worry, madame," replied the king of detectives in a loud voice. "He won't be hurting you."

"What!" the excellent woman started up. "You're not Moniseur?"

"Have no fear," the great bloodhound hastened to declare. "I'm a friend who is saving you from great danger and preventing you from being compromised in a business whose consequences could be worse than tiresome for you."

"This isn't possible? I'm dreaming!" murmured Scholastic.

Chantecoq, who had discovered the switch placed at the head of the bed, turned on the light.

At the sight of those two men with a grave but benevolent expression, standing at her bedside, the poor old woman shuddered.

In the grip of intense shock and joining her hands, she said with dread, "Really, you don't want to murder us?"

"That's not exactly our job," grunted the king of detectives. And he added, "Come on, madame, cast off this emotion that we apologise for having provoked. Once again, don't be afraid."

Overwhelmed by her visitor, the servant fixed him with a gaze that was still anguished. Then she stammered, "I recognise you. You came to see the professor. You went out with him. You're Monsieur... What is it now again? You're called..."

"Chantecoq."

"That's it!"

"And here's my friend Monsieur Lereni, the chief of police."

"The police!" the old woman started. "But I've committed no crime; I've never wronged anyone; I have a son who's a priest, and vicar of Vannes Cathedral. You can gather information on me..."

Interrupting the flow of those protestations whose accent of perfect sincerity would have been enough to dissipate all suspicion, the great bloodhound replied, "Don't torment yourself so, madame. You're not at fault. And you will never be troubled, so long as you don't hesitate to tell us, Monsieur Lereni and I, the whole truth and nothing but the truth."

Tearful, Scholastic cried, "Has some misfortune befallen my master?"

"No, no," Chantecoq affirmed sharply.

"Yes," the vicar's mother was obstinate. "You don't want to tell me, but I'm sure of it. Is it his own fault? I foresaw that. By dint of handling dangerous drugs, he ended up poisoning himself."

Happy to observe that the servant was answering in advance the questions that he had intended to put to her, Chantecoq continued. "What are these dangerous drugs of which you speak?"

"I have no idea. All I can tell you is that one day, we were still in Rosporden, he showed me a little glass tube which contained some liquid as clear as water. And he said to me, 'With that, I have all I need to kill a hundred people!' Then, I ran out, I was so afraid!"

Chantecoq replied, "You didn't think to ask him what use he intended for this terrible poison?"

"My word, no," replied Scholastic demurely. "He's such a noble man that I didn't think for one moment he could make use of it against the world!"

And, ready to burst into tears, she added, "So, he's poisoned himself?"

"No, madame, I promise you, I even give you my word of honour."

"And I too," added the chief of police.

"So," asked the servant, "what are you doing here, both of you, in the middle of the night?"

"We'll tell you shortly," replied Chantecoq. "But beforehand, I'd like you to answer honestly the question that I'm about to ask you."

"Speak, monsieur, you can relax. It's not I who will seek to mislead you, first, because a priest's mother can not lie; then, because you both seem to me to be such honest people that, now, I'm no longer afraid of you and I even trust you."

"You're right, madame," declared Chantecoq. "Far from causing you the slightest harm, the chief of police and I, we're completely disposed to help you, in the event, highly unlikely in any case, that you might be accused!"

"Accused? Of what, my God!" cried Scholastic.

"Madame," replied Chantecoq in his persuasive voice, "just now you shouted out, talking about your master: 'so, he's poisoned himself?' You seemed to indicate you feared he might have committed suicide?"

"I've feared that for a long time," replied the servant with all desirable clarity, "especially after Madame's death. He no longer wanted to live, and my deceased husband and I asked ourselves if he would ever be consoled."

"However, he forgot," insinuated Monsieur Lereni.

"No," replied Scholastic. "He's still thinking of his poor wife. She was so beautiful! He loved her so much! Then, at times, that gives him episodes…"

"What episodes?"

"At night, he suddenly wakes up, dresses, and goes for walks in the apartment, heaving deep sighs… Once, I found him at two o'clock in the morning in his lounge sitting on an armchair, his head in his hands, sobbing.

"He didn't see me, he didn't hear me, and I didn't want to reveal myself to him, because I thought that might anger him to realise I had discovered him like that, he who is so proud!

"Another night, when I was not sleeping, he came into my room. Then, surprised, I said to him, 'Monsieur, what do you want?'

"He didn't answer me. He had his eyes closed and he was walking like a ghost. He went out just as he came, without opening his eyelids, without unclenching his teeth, and yet without bumping into any furniture.

"I followed him, because I was afraid some misfortune would befall him. He returned to his office; he locked himself in. It's strange all the same, gentlemen, and yet that happened just as I'm telling you; I'm inventing nothing, I'm telling you the truth, as you asked me to, monsieur, nothing but the truth.

"But that's not all: the day before yesterday, I was in the middle of tidying his bedroom, this was in the morning, and he was in his office, all alone, still handling his glass tubes.

"I believed there was a knock at the door; I wasn't quite sure of it; I'm quite hard of hearing; but as I didn't want to leave people on the landing, I went at once to go and see.

"In order to get into the hallway, I had to cross the professor's office. As soon as he saw me, he locked his tubes in a drawer and began to shout at me, 'You could knock before entering.'

"He seemed very angry. I had never seen him like that, in the almost twenty-five years that I've been in his service. I made my best apologies. He sent me out for a walk. For nothing, I believe that he would have jostled me, he who is so good to me!

"When I tried to come back to finish my work, he had locked himself in and I didn't see him again until lunchtime. Then he said in a much softer tone, 'You mustn't judge me if I'm a bit of a bully this morning. When I'm working, I can't bear to be disturbed, especially without warning…'

"This language surprised me a bit, because I'd happened to enter the office many times when Monsieur was in the middle of writing or was bent over his books, and he had never offered me any reproach… I said nothing; I continued my little routine as usual.

"I'm telling you all this, gentlemen, because I promised to hide nothing from you. Now, would you be so good as to reassure me completely on my boss's fate? He has always been so good towards me, and I'm so attached to him that, if some misfortune has befallen him, I believe that I would never recover from it!"

"You're too brave a woman," replied Chantecoq, "for me to inflict the slightest hurt on you, but you're also too honest a person for me not to begin to open your eyes on your master. It may be that he has been very good to you, and even with regard to other people.

"As to his genius, I won't dispute that for a moment. That man should certainly have been one of the most illustrious in France and even in the whole world."

"Isn't he just, monsieur?" Scholastic beamed.

"Unfortunately," Chantecoq continued, "all the troubles and deceit he experienced in the course of his career have scrambled his nervous system considerably.

"The death of his wife and, perhaps further, the circumstances which preceded it, managed to disturb his mental equilibrium; a cerebral lesion was produced in him and, for a long time now, Professor Courtil, my poor lady,

169

has lost if not all his reason, but at least a good portion of it.

"This is what we call a maniac. These maniacs are the most dangerous of all. Most of the time, their state isn't at all suspicious, and it's impossible to prevent them from harm.

"I beg your pardon for causing you this distress, but I can't hide from you further that you must wait here for some serious and even extremely serious news.

"If I have one piece of advice, I believe you'd do best to return to Brittany to be near your son."

Poor Scholastic, holding back her tears with great difficulty, cried, "I think I understand: poor Monsieur is going to be locked up in a madhouse…"

Chantecoq replied, "For that, we need to know where to find him."

"What! He's not here?"

"No," replied the king of detectives. "Just now, he was in his office; I was speaking with him, when he stood up and headed for a door that he opened, then he vanished. It was impossible for me to find him again."

As Scholastic was rolling her frightened eyes, Chantecoq asked her, "Have you ever noticed in this apartment other entrances than those which lead to the landing?"

"My God! No, monsieur."

"You're absolutely sure of that?"

"Oh! Yes, very sure, completely sure."

Suddenly Scholastic cried out, "So long as he's not thrown himself out of the window!"

"That's impossible," confirmed the king of detectives, "in the cabinet he entered, there was no kind of opening, other than that by which he entered."

"Oh! Yes, the black cabinet," declared Scholastic. "Then I

no longer understand, I don't know any more! Oh! Good gentlemen, all this has given me a fever. I don't dare stay alone in this house any longer."

"Be calm," cried Chantecoq, "you're under our protection, and nothing bad will happen to you. You go and get dressed in peace. The chief of police will leave one of his agents here, who, when we've left, will remain nearby. In this fashion, you'll have nothing to fear.

"Don't worry, we won't abandon you. Quite the reverse."

And, addressing himself to Lereni, the great detective said, "Now, my dear, let's leave this good lady to gather her wits and return to the professor's office."

The king of detectives and the policeman hurried back to the office from which Météor had not budged.

"Nothing new?" asked Chantecoq.

"Nothing, boss."

"You heard no unexpected noise?"

"None."

"We've just seen Madame Scholastic. She gave us no information capable of putting us on the Ladykiller's trail; however, what she did tell us only confirmed that this monster is a maniac, just as we already suspected. Now, my dear Lereni, I'm going to ask you for a favour."

"Please do, my dear master."

"Météor was able to take down the number of the car which took Professor Courtil away. Thanks to that number, so long as it's not been falsified, it would be child's play for you, my dear friend, to find out its owner's name."

Météor passed to Monsieur Lereni the paper on which he had written the mysterious car's number.

Lereni picked up the telephone, which was placed on the

171

scholar's desk, and he asked for a connection with his secretary.

When he obtained it, he spoke into the device. "Is that you, Clermier? Director Lereni here. Could you find out the owner's name for vehicle registration 31.27-RB? As soon as you have it, send it to me; wait while I find out the number."

Chantecoq, who was gifted with a formidable memory, supplied it. "78-91".

Monsieur Lereni repeated the number and hung up the phone.

"In the meantime," decided the king of detectives, "I believe we ought to conduct a little search, thanks to which we might be able to obtain some advantageous results."

"I was going to suggest that," declared Monsieur Lereni.

"You, my little Météor," continued the great bloodhound, "I'll ask you to go back to the hallway and watch the door. We can't be too careful, especially when we're taking decisive action."

Météor obeyed at once and left the room.

Chantecoq took from his pocket a roll of cloth from which hung some keys and hooks of all shapes and sizes.

"There we are," Monsieur Lereni said with a smile, "A true burglar's toolkit."

Chantecoq replied, "It is, indeed, the arsenal belonging to an international jewel thief who I succeeded in catching a few years ago. Only, I employ it in a quite different manner.

"Thanks to this precious collection and the knowledge of how to make use of it, I know hardly any lock that's capable of resisting me."

Chantecoq approached Professor Courtil's desk and, choosing from his roll a strange little instrument, which combined at once the shape of an ordinary key with that of a crowbar and a monkey wrench, after having adapted it to the size of the lock that he wanted to open, he slid it delicately into the opening and, at once, without the slightest effort, without the tiniest difficulty, he pulled the drawer towards him.

It was full of small wooden rectangular boxes, which all bore a label on which was written some figures, whose meaning was known only to the professor. Chantecoq picked up one of these boxes and opened it.

It contained ten or so tubes containing a colourless liquid, lying on cotton wool.

"There's not a shadow of a doubt," said the king of detectives, "these ampoules contain the poison in which the Ladykiller soaks the needles with which he pricks his victims.

"My dear Lereni, you only have to grab one of these boxes and send it to police headquarters, where they will do the necessary. It will furnish us with absolute proof that Professor Courtil really is the mysterious assassin you've been pursuing for several weeks."

"It will only remain for us to arrest him," observed Monsieur Lereni. "I imagine now that will be less difficult than I first feared."

And the king of detectives added, "Let's continue our research, while we're waiting for the car's number…"

Chantecoq and Monsieur Lereni continued their investigations and discovered several documents that they evidently found of great interest, because they hurried to place them inside a large yellow envelope they found on the professor's desk, and then sealed it with wax.

As they were finishing this operation, the telephone rang. Lereni picked up the device: it was his secretary who was sending him the name and the address of the car spotted by

Météor: he was called Will Strimer and he lived at 67, Avenue de Breteuil.

"Will Strimer!" exclaimed Chantecoq, to whom Monsieur Lereni communicated these details. "I know that name. He's a so-called American detective, a notorious scoundrel and I'm astonished he's still in France, after all the shady and even improper acts for which he's accountable."

The chief of police replied, not without a certain melancholy. "You know, my dear master, how difficult it is for an honest Frenchman to visit America. You'll learn nothing, alas, if I observe how difficult it is to get a dishonest American out of France."

"You're right," observed Chantecoq, "but, in any case, he won't be long in facing his reckoning. Now, the only unresolved question in my mind is cleared up in a dazzling fashion. I was wondering, indeed, how Professor Courtil could so well know the names, personalities and, I'll add, the guilt of all the adulterous women he sent into the next world.

"I naturally assumed he had an accomplice. Eh! By Jove! Here he is: Will Strimer, this base American detective, just the man for all the dirty jobs and ready to commit any infamies.

"What still bothers me a little, is that this bully must not have granted his services to the Ladykiller freely. He must have made him pay very dearly for them."

"By the head," stressed Lereni.

Chantecoq continued. "After the declarations Scholastic made to Météor during a previous investigation, declarations which were faithfully transmitted to me as my secretary always does, and whose sincerity I have no reason to doubt, Professor Courtil has a fortune of around one hundred thousand francs in rent.

"As you know, my dear friend, in these times, such a capital sum doesn't get you very far, so long as this Courtil, in order to satisfy his dreadful mania, resolved to sacrifice his last centime to it; it's a question with which the prosecutor will have to worry himself later. The main thing is to get our hands on the murderer and his accomplice. I'm asking you, my dear Lereni, to let me act freely. I promise to deliver the two culprits very shortly. I'll keep my word.

"In order that there be no misunderstanding, or surprise, answer my call only if it's *Cocorico* who asks for you.

"Now, we have nothing more to do here. It's certain Professor Courtil is not close to coming home. However, I'll leave Météor on guard. I'll ask you to be so kind as to replace him as soon as possible with one of your best inspectors, to whom you'll give all necessary instructions."

"Very well, my dear master."

"I'll now launch my hunt for the man, or the two men, of whom we must rid society at all costs."

"And I," replied the chief of police, "what am I going to do in all this?"

"Go home and go to bed quietly; sleep like a man with a clean conscience and who I hope will be awoken, if he sleeps until seven o'clock in the morning, by a loud and triumphant *cocorico*.

"Then, come running so I can hand over to you one of the most interesting quarries which has been given to me to pursue throughout the whole course of my long career."

"I see, my dear master," said Monsieur Lereni, "that I was right to come to you. You are, and you always will be, our master."

"My dear," replied the king of detectives, "you didn't

need to pay me this compliment for me to declare to you how delighted I was to do this service for you. Be assured, each time that I spot the opportunity, I'll grasp it with the greatest eagerness. Now, let's get moving, because I have a fair few things to sort out before daybreak. It's already one o'clock in the morning."

They both went back to the hallway. Chantecoq warned his secretary that Scholastic, dressed as though she was ready to go out, was going to join them.

"You're going to watch over that brave woman," he added, "and over the rest, until the chief of police can have you relieved from your post. Then go straight to Avenue de Verzy, don't go to sleep, and await a telephone call from me in my office, which will tell you what you have to do."

"Good, boss," agreed Météor.

Chantecoq and Lereni went back down to the street. The great bloodhound headed towards his Talbot, which was parked a few metres from there, near the pavement.

Chantecoq suggested to his friend, "Would you like me to give you a lift home?"

Monsieur Lereni refused. "There's no point," he said. "I live just by here, on Rue de Rennes. I don't want to take up a single moment of your precious time."

Chantecoq opened the door of his car which he had locked, and left at high speed.

He reached the docks. When he pulled up in front of Gare d'Orsay, he stopped at the space where the taxis were parked during the day, and, closing his blinds, he climbed over the bench on which he was sitting, lifted up the car's rear cushions, which contained a secret coffer that he opened at once and inside which he plunged his hand.

A few moments later, Chantecoq returned to the wheel

under a different guise. It was no longer Chantecoq in the flesh but a man with the respectable appearance of a provincial notary, who seemed bewildered at finding himself in the capital. He wore no sideburns, as did so many 19th Century legal clerks, but quite a voluminous beard, or rather badly-groomed; the moustache, in particular, seemed to have sprouted in every direction.

In any case, one thing that could be confirmed, he was completely unrecognisable.

He drove his car to a garage neighbouring Gare d'Orsay and he hoped it would be kept there until the following day.

From there, he went to the Gare d'Orsay hotel, asked for a room with a bathroom and a telephone communicating with the town. While speaking to the night receptionist, he had, without appearing to mean anything by it, toyed with a wallet stuffed with banknotes.

His request was immediately granted. He was asked if he had any luggage, and he answered, "I left my suitcase on the train by mistake, but I took the necessary steps, and I hope I'll recover it tomorrow morning."

He didn't insist, and was immediately led away by a porter. Under the name of Monsieur Josset, notary in Saint-Jean-La-Poterie, near to Redon (Ille-et-Vilaine) they went to the room that had been reserved for him. There, after locking the door and taking rapid stock of the room, he consulted a telephone directory placed on a table, grabbed the telephone and asked for the Ségur number 52-47, that of the detective Will Strimer.

Chantecoq wasn't long in hearing from the other end of the line a voice which hailed him, with a strong American accent, "Hello! Who's that? Hello! Who's after me?"

Chantecoq replied, "Master Josset, a notary from Brittany.

177

Are you Monsieur Will Strimer?"

"Yes, yes, that's me. What do you want?"

"I've been the victim of a serious theft. Could you come and pick me up, because I can, right now, give you the necessary clues which will allow you to uncover the robber or rather the robberess at once.

"Though it's very late, I would be particularly grateful for your trouble. I'll start by telling you I'm ready to give you a cheque for ten thousand francs up front. You see the case is worth the trouble?"

"Where are you right now?" the American asked.

"At the hotel at Gare d'Orsay[13], where I've just been despoiled in the most extraordinary fashion. You only have to ask for Master Josset, notary. In any case, I'm in room number 121."

The American detective, or rather gumshoe, the snitch for hire that he was, replied, "I'll be with you in half an hour."

Indeed, Will Strimer, not suspecting for a moment the trap that the world's greatest bloodhound was setting for him, felt attracted by the powerful bait of a doubtless highly compromising adventure in which an honourable provincial scrivener had got himself mixed up, and who, to head off a scandal, would be ready to make any sacrifice.

---

[13] The source text says "Gare d'Orléans" here. Gare d'Orléans isn't even in *Paris*, but the Loire. Gare d'Orsay opened in 1900 to connect Southwest France with Paris, but short platforms made it obsolete for long-distance services by 1939. It was used, among other things, as a film set for the Orson Welles 1962 adaptation of Kafka's *The Trial*, before finally being converted into the art gallery Musée d'Orsay which opened in 1986. The hotel that Chantecoq describes here remained open until the 1970s.

So, half an hour later, he arrived at the Gare d'Orsay hotel, where Chantecoq was preparing to set a trap into which Will was going to charge headlong, because he wasn't gifted with great finesse, and only his absolute lack of scruples, and his procedures stripped of the most elementary probity, had won him success among a clientele which was not exactly the most discerning as to the choice of those whom it took into their service.

The American went to the front desk to ask the night manager for Monsieur Josset. The manager took an internal telephone and asked the fake notary if he was happy to receive Monsieur Will Strimer.

The response was naturally affirmative, and guided by a porter, the American detective took the lift. Some moments later, he knocked at our national Chantecoq's bedroom door. He, as we've already seen and as we're going to see again, was a master in the art of composing the characters to whom he distributed his roles.

Admirably disguised to such an extent that, in spite of himself, it was impossible to notice he was dressed up in a fake beard and wig, he stepped forward with his hands outstretched, towards the American detective who, while looking him up and down disdainfully, was saying to himself,

"Here's one who's not going to weigh heavily on my hands."

"Monsieur detective," began the pretend Josset, "how grateful I am to you for coming running at my call, because you're going to save more than my life, but my honour."

"I'm not promising anything," replied the detective with a mid-Atlantic nasal twang.

Adopting a self-important tone, he said, "First, before beginning the slightest discussion, I'd like to know your

179

reasons for contacting me over and above all the others."

Without the slightest hesitation, Chantecoq replied. "Following my misadventure which has just befallen me and I'll tell you about in a moment, I had them bring me a directory and I looked for the address of the private detective who lived nearest here. It happened to be you. That's why I called you, because as you'll see, things need to be managed very carefully. Here it is, then…"

Chantecoq was about to begin the tale he had already imagined in every detail. But with a brusque, even brutal gesture, which demonstrated just how much he was lacking any kind of education beneath his appearance of a proper and well raised gentleman, Will Strimer interrupted, saying, "One more question. Why not go to your country's police force?"

"Because, as I just told you, my honour is at stake."

Taking on a strict air, Will cried out, "Would you by any chance have committed an indiscretion?"

"Me?" protested the fake notary with the talent of a marvellous actor, "Me, an indiscretion? Ah! Monsieur, it's clear you don't know me. For more than three centuries, the Jossets have been notaries, father and son, at Saint-Jean-la-Potterie. All the inhabitants of that little town, modest and industrious, as well as for ten leagues around, will tell you, 'Never has a Josset committed the slightest error or inflicted the smallest wrong on his neighbour!'"

Entirely fooled, Will Strimer replied. "Forgive me, monsieur, but, before taking on a case, especially when it's presented in such an unexpected fashion, I always make it a principle to inform myself as much as possible about the people with whom I'm dealing."

"With me, you can rest easy," replied the king of

detectives.

"I'm persuaded of that, and I hope you won't hold my personal indiscretion against me."

"I approve of it completely," Chantecoq declared gravely. "These scruples do you credit and show me how right I was to trust you. Myself, if I was a private detective like you, I would not act any differently. But, forgive me, Monsieur Will Strimer, I didn't notice I had left you standing."

And, waving to an armchair placed near a table, he said, "Please do sit down."

The American sat down in the armchair where he sat back with the lack of inhibition which characterises certain of his compatriots who, when they find themselves in France, believe it to be good form to conduct themselves as men without breeding.

Chantecoq took his place on a chair opposite him and he began.

"For a long time, I was not happy at home. I had married for love, a young orphan from Nantes, with no fortune, but with whom I was hopelessly smitten. I soon noticed, but too late, alas, that my love had not found the slightest echo in the heart of she who had become my wife. But, as I cared for her above all else, I resolved to do anything to keep her near me.

"Thinking that she wasn't having much fun in Saint-Jean-la-Potterie and that she needed distractions, I brought her from time to time, as often as possible, to Nantes where we went together to the theatre, the cinema, and even to the music-hall.

"I confess to you, this type of leisure offers only a mediocre attraction for me. But that wasn't enough for Colette… I had forgotten to tell you that my wife's called Colette."

"That's not a problem," said the American, taking from his pocket a pipe which he began to stuff without even asking his host's permission.

Chantecoq, or rather Master Josset, continued. "Soon, she started talking about Paris. Paris was the object of her dreams. For her, it was only there that she could live happily.

"One day, she declared to me, to my deep stupefaction, that, if I didn't sell my study and if I wasn't going to settle with her in the capital, she would go… that's it precisely, monsieur, she would go all alone. She would leave me there in my corner, sad and bereft.

"It was in vain that I tried to convince Colette to reverse her decision. There was nothing to be done, as you can to observe. I'm much older than her and the thought of losing that adorable child, who had come to brighten my ripe age with her radiant youth gave me such dark ideas that she ended up making me think, if she left me, I would kill myself. Better then to go with her.

"Some time later, I sold my business at a very good price. Adding a few hundred thousand francs to the personal fortune I possess, I had the wherewithal to live in Paris, if not grandly, but, at the very least, lacking nothing.

"My intention was to set up or to buy a legal consultation office, which would have added to my income, because we provincial notaries, we're mocked sometimes, but we know how to sort ourselves out, even better than our city colleagues. The art of chicanery has no secrets for us.

"Let's move on though, I'm getting to the result. While waiting to transfer my capital to a Paris bank, I brought with me a sum of one hundred thousand francs, which I prudently stashed in the lining of my jacket.

"We took the train this morning. Colette seemed to be in

a delightful mood; we ate lunch in the diner car. It was poor fare; but Colette, finding everything exquisite, I didn't want to shatter her illusions, and I was in ecstasy myself over the boiled eggs and slices of veal that were as thin as an air current and to which a few lettuce leaves had been added.

"When we arrived here, Colette was literally radiant; we dined at the hotel and from there, at once, she wanted us to go and see the show at Folies-Bergère.

"I didn't want to argue with her over so little. We took a taxi which took us to the famous establishment on Rue Richer and we spent an excellent evening there. Colette was so joyful, and I was so satisfied to see her showing her happiness like that, that I suggested we have supper in a Montmartre nightclub.

"You see, monsieur, I was prepared to make every sacrifice. But to my great surprise, Colette refused, and calling me her darling for the first time, she said she'd rather go back to the hotel.

"In the taxi which took us there, she leaned against me, rested her head against my shoulder, provoking a kiss that she didn't begrudge me and which she accepted without constraint. I was swimming in happiness. I imagined I was perhaps about to experience the pleasures I had believed forbidden to me forever and I thanked Paris, that great Paris, with its glittering lights, that Paris of instinct, that I had cursed so many times, and that today I adored; I was blessing it, for I had the unwise gullibility to imagine it was going to open the gates of heaven to me."

Chantecoq had launched this tirade with such a note of sincerity and was observing such a natural attitude that, more and more convinced he was dealing with a pear who was asking only to be picked, Will Strimer, inhaling large puffs of

183

smoke, was already estimating the profit he would extract from the case at five hundred thousand francs.

Chantecoq, who had got his breath back, continued. "Now, I'm getting to the drama, to the catastrophe. I wanted to be brief, but I consider it my duty to give you all the details."

The American gave a nod of approval. Then he said, "The case being worth the effort, I'm happy to listen to everything, just as I am to do everything."

Chantecoq continued. "On returning to the hotel, I began by removing my overcoat, my jacket, which I left lying over the back of a chair, and I spent a few moments in the bathroom.

"When I returned a few minutes later, Colette had disappeared. 'Oh no!' I said to myself, 'what's become of her?' Where had she gone? I thought she was hiding, to give me a fright, when I noticed my jacket on the ground. I was instinctively anxious; I picked it up and noticed the lining was ripped open and the thousand franc notes I had sewn into that hiding place had vanished.

"I remained stunned for a few moments; then, gathering my wits, I cast an eye over my jacket, dangling pathetically between my hands, and I noticed, pinned to its lining, an envelope which I grabbed and opened at once.

"That envelope contained a letter composed as follows…

Monsieur,

I've had enough of living with you. I love a great artist and I'm going to restart my life with him.

I'm taking from you a sum which, for certain, does not represent the value of renting out my person for the four years I've had to endure your conjugal tyranny. I consider myself quits with you, and I trust you will

call it quits with me!
Farewell!
Colette.

Chantecoq continued, still inhabiting his character more than ever. "If I'm asking you to launch yourself into the fugitive's pursuit, it's not that I still want her back; but I would like to get my money back, and I desire that so much more because the great artist with whom she claims to be restarting her life, is none other than a lowlife dancehall gigolo she knew in Nantes and with whom she is obviously more smitten than ever.

"Now, I've nothing more to tell you. It's up to you to give me an answer, if you'll accept the mission I'm entrusting to you."

"I accept," declared the American.

"Thank you," the notary replied. "Now will you be so good as to give me your terms?"

Brutally, in the American manner, Will Strimer decreed, "Write a cheque for seven hundred dollars, by way of deposit, and I'll get to work at once."

"Seven hundred dollars," replied the fake scrivener, "in France, even these days, we have kept the habit of counting in francs."

"Very well! That makes around eighteen thousand francs," the yankee detective conceded with a disdainful air.

Chantecoq replied, "I'll get my cheque book… Forgive me, I'm so flummoxed by the catastrophe that has struck me that I can't even find my own head."

The American remained unmoving and silent, clearly demonstrating he had decided to wait.

Affecting a more and more agitated attitude, the king of

detectives began rummaging through his jacket pockets, while saying, "Just so long as she's taken that as well! In fact, no, that wouldn't do her any good. She's incapable of imitating my signature.

"Unless she wanted to play a nasty trick on me. With creatures like that, do we ever know how far things might go?"

Suddenly the great bloodhound let out a cry of triumph. "Ah! Here it is."

Then, returning brusquely to Will Strimer who, stretched out in his armchair, was waiting and smoking his pipe, his feet up on a small table opposite him, he said in a worried, almost weepy tone,

"Tell me, monsieur: if you do find my wife, as I'm sure you will, don't hurt her!"

"Me, hurt her!" the American was astonished. "I've no intention of doing so."

"However…" Chantecoq objected timidly.

"However, what?" his guest asked.

"I'd been told… but I daren't repeat it to you."

"You're wrong to be embarrassed around me."

"I don't believe a word of it, however."

"Very well then! Spit it out, quickly, at once."

"I was told…"

The skilled bloodhound stopped again.

The American said, "That I was brutal in carrying out my duties?"

"Oh! Not at all…"

"Then what?" The Yankee was beginning to get annoyed.

"Oh! It's this nasty rumour going around. Simply, I was told it was you signalling to the Ladykiller the adulterous

186

women he was then killing."

At this phrase the king of detectives had spoken, lowering his head and half-closing his eyes, as though he feared to meet those of his companion, the American jumped out of his seat.

Chantecoq had struck home. Will Strimer cried out. "Now I see: you're an agent of the Sûreté and you want to lead me into an ambush. Well! Too bad for you!"

Chantecoq had manoeuvred himself in such a way that he was positioned between Courtil's accomplice and the door, which led to the landing.

Taking on a flabbergasted and frightened attitude, he babbled, "Too bad for me? I don't understand!"

"Well, you're going to understand," growled the rogue, brandishing a Browning he had taken from the back pocket of his trousers.

And he said, "Hands up!"

"Hands up? Why?" the fake scrivener asked in a tremulous voice.

The American retorted, "Because if you don't obey me, I'll blow your brains out."

"Not possible?"

"You have one minute."

"You won't do that."

"Oh! You think?"

The American pointed his gun at Chantecoq's forehead, barely a metre away from him.

The king of detectives didn't budge an inch. And, suddenly taking on an ironic tone and a provocative attitude, he said, "You can fire, Monsieur Will Strimer, I'm perfectly at ease. There are no cartridges in that weapon."

"No cartridges?"

"Oh no," said the world's greatest bloodhound calmly. And he continued. "I'm very sure, given that this Browning is my own, and yours is in my pocket.

"You must confess it's quite rare to meet a provincial notary with such talent for sleight-of-hand."

Believing the fake scrivener was bluffing, the American detective pulled the trigger. But the gun didn't go off. He looked at the weapon. His opponent was right, it wasn't his.

He threw it aside, in a gesture of rage. Furious, he shouted, "To pull off such a trick you must be either a cop or a thief."

And he added with a defiant tone, "But you don't know who you're dealing with."

"You neither."

Overcome with fury, Will Strimer tried to hurl himself on Chantecoq. As always, he was prepared.

With a magisterial left hook, he sent his adversary crashing to the ground. Then, arming himself with the Browning he had so craftily pinched, he said to him, "It's my turn to say to you: hands up! Or I will shoot. And you must know this gun is loaded, since it belongs to you."

"*All right!*" said the American who, flat on the ground, painfully climbed to his knees and, with difficulty, raised his arms in the air.

"You," he murmured, "you're an ace?"

"One does what one can."

In a voice which was gradually regaining its strength, but while keeping the position that the greatest policeman of our age had ordered him to take, he added, "I know only one detective capable of pulling off such a feat…"

"What's his name?" asked our friend.

"Chantecoq!"

"And if I told you that I am he…"

"I would answer that it's very possible."

"You could equally tell yourself it's certain."

And, pulling off his beard and his wig with a flourish, he added with the calm that allowed him his extraordinary mastery, "Best I continue this interview under my true appearance."

"You decked me!" grumbled the American.

"I did what I could," said the Frenchman with a smile.

"Between colleagues, that's not on."

"Allow me, Monsieur Will Strimer. We hold such different conceptions of our profession that I refuse you categorically the right to invoke any kind of professional solidarity between us. Now, after these lengthy preliminaries, I intend to move fast. I have only one question to ask you anyway: *How much does Professor Courtil pay for each new scalp you bring him?*"

"Each scalp?" replied the American, pretending not to grasp the meaning of Chantecoq's words.

He clarified. "Each woman…"

"To answer that, I'd need to be acquainted with this professor."

"Oh, so you don't know him?"

"No."

"I'm warning you that you're setting foot on rather dangerous territory there…"

"I assure you…"

"You know the Ladykiller very well, whom you came to fetch in your car this evening, to drive him to the Ministry of Commerce, where there was a grand reception and where he

189

made two new victims! Then you drove him back home.

"There's no point in denying it! My secretary spotted your car's number; that's what allowed me to spot you, and set this little booby trap. Acknowledge that you hadn't stolen it!"

The American kept quiet. He was beaten. For him it was now just a case of getting out of the whole business as easily as possible.

Chantecoq was too gifted a psychologist not to guess what was going on inside his head.

He said to himself, "I have him and, soon, he'll show himself to be as loquacious as he has been reserved up to now!"

Aloud, he continued. "I'll therefore repeat my question: how much did the Ladykiller pay you for each victim that you brought to him."

"Monsieur Chantecoq, I assure you that never..."

"Don't try to deny it. I won't believe you. Because I know how it all happened and I'll tell you.

"One fine day, you received a visit from Professor Courtil, who said this: 'Monsieur Detective, in your line of work, it must happen frequently, on the request of husbands who believe they have been betrayed, that you follow unfaithful spouses with a view to catching them in the act. I'm asking if you could then furnish me the name, the address and the description of all such culprits; in return for which I'll reward you handsomely!'

"Without even asking for an explanation of this offer, which must have inspired if not suspicions then at least some vague worries, you accepted at once. Because you had, and you still have, a pressing need for money.

"The nightclubs of Montmartre and of Montparnasse cost dearly. Let's move on. One day, you noticed - this was

190

fatal - that all the young women you had flagged up to Professor Courtil were disappearing, one after the other, in a manner as similar as it was swift.

"A little emotional, despite your instinct which is above all based on a total lack of scruples, you went to find the Ladykiller. You questioned him! He responded to you very clearly. Because he was waiting for it, and he had been prepared for some time.

"Here is the substance of his declaration: 'It is I, indeed, who is wiping out all the women you send to me. If you denounce me, I'll affirm you were in league with me and I'll drag you into sharing my fate. Because you can be sure I'll be believed!'

"That's pretty much what he said to you, isn't it? You're not answering? We're in agreement! Caught in the gears, through fear more than cupidity, you continued to furnish the executioner with his victims. You're a wretch, Will Strimer!

"But I don't want to bring Professor Courtil's accomplice to justice, but to get hold of the murderer and put him out of harm's way. Certainly you have a terrible responsibility. If you were judged at the same time as the Ladykiller, I wonder if you would manage to save your neck? In any case, you'd certainly be condemned to a life sentence of hard labour."

At this threat, the American couldn't repress a shudder. Chantecoq continued. "One word from me, or rather one telephone call, and you'd be put away immediately. I won't do it, but on one condition: you immediately tell me where Professor Courtil is to be found."

"I don't know."

"Joker!"

"I assure you I have no idea…"

"We'll see about that."

While keeping his Browning trained on the American, Chantecoq headed to the telephone.

"What are you going to do?" asked Will Strimer feverishly, still kneeling with his arms in the air.

"Alert the police…"

"For pity's sake."

"Ah! You're deflating!"

"No, but… I…"

Implacably the king of detectives reached for the telephone. Losing his head completely, mad as a cornered beast, obeying a reflexive defensive instinct, the American detective sprung to his feet and launched himself towards Chantecoq.

He, instead of slaughtering him with a shot from the Browning, contented himself with dealing him a terrible uppercut which knocked him out.

"And now," he said, "we're going to have a bit of fun…"

He went towards his overcoat that he had thrown on the bed and took from one of its pockets one of the two metallic boxes that we saw him bring in.

He opened it and took hold of a silk cord, with which he began to truss up the American detective, who was out cold.

Then, as a precautionary measure, he gagged him with his handkerchief and, heading again to the telephone, he was about to operate it, when the bell rang.

He picked up the receiver and listened. A voice was heard at the other end of the line.

Chantecoq, who had every kind of total recall, including that of hearing, immediately recognised the professor's voice.

"Hello!" said Courtil. "Is that you, Strimer?"

In an instant perfect imitation of Will's accent and

intonations, the great French bloodhound replied, "It's me."

"I was beginning to worry about your absence, I was afraid you'd fallen into some trap."

"No, it's going very well, as it happens. I just found you a new client. Come and meet me at once at the hotel on the Quai d'Orsay. Ask to speak to Master Josset, notary. I'll give the front desk all the necessary instructions for you to be received immediately. Just give your name and you'll be brought to me at once."

"Understood, but don't fear…"

"I'm completely relaxed."

"Then, see you soon!"

"See you soon!"

Chantecoq hung up the receiver. He was wearing his smile for great days or rather for beautiful nights of victory.

The manhunt had not been of long duration; now he was no longer pursuing the game: the game was coming itself to be taken in the trap.

He was on the point of launching himself on to the telephone, to ask for Monsieur Lereni's number and to wake him with a triumphant *cocorico*.

But he thought, "Let him sleep a while longer, I'll call him only when I've completely fulfilled the promise I made him. Also, I wouldn't mind, not through self-love, but through professional curiosity, to have one last meeting face to face with the Ladykiller. I've an idea that this final conversation still holds some surprises for me."

Going to the American who was beginning to return to his senses, but was still completely immobilised by the gag and the bonds bestowed upon him, the king of detectives grabbed him with vigorous arms and dragged him over to the bathroom, stretching him over the bottom of the bathtub, hiding him under a robe, and leaving the door open so as to keep watch over his prisoner. Then he returned to the bedroom and murmured,

"While I wait for the professor, I believe I've got time to smoke a good pipe…"

12 WHERE IT'S OBSERVED THAT SPLIT PERSONALITY THEORY IS A SCIENTIFIC TRUTH WE SHOULDN'T DISCOUNT

Chantecoq picked up the hotel's internal telephone and warned the concierge on duty that as soon as Professor Courtil introduced himself, he should show him to the bedroom.

Then, as he had promised himself, he stuffed and lit his pipe. After reflecting for a few minutes, sending towards the ceiling the large clouds of blueish smoke that he was drawing from his peace pipe, Chantecoq put his jacket back on, replaced his wig, reattached the false beard to his chin and went to take from the second metallic box a strangely-shaped pistol which he hid in his jacket pocket.

Then he installed himself comfortably in an armchair, and waited patiently for events to unfold, or rather for Professor Courtil, who was not long in announcing his presence.

Barely half an hour after the end of the duel between the great French detective and the pitiful American detective, there was a knock at the door.

"Come in!" said the bloodhound at once.

A porter appeared, announcing, "Professor Courtil."

Then he stood aside, to allow the scholar to enter the room. He withdrew at once, leaving our drama's two protagonists face to face.

On noticing that the notary Josset was alone, the chemist displayed a certain surprise.

So Chantecoq hastened to declare, "Professor, don't worry yourself on Monsieur Will Strimer's account. He had to pop out for a few minutes, but he won't be long and he asked me, while awaiting his return, to keep you company."

A little worried, Courtil wondered, "What a strange idea Strimer had to make me come here and then leave me alone with this individual whom I don't know from Adam. He seems a decent chap, but one never knows, does one?"

Interrupting these thoughts, the false scrivener invited him to sit in the armchair he had been occupying just a few moments before.

Professor Courtil complied, visibly disturbed. His disquiet was expressed in these words:

"Do you think, monsieur, that Monsieur Strimer will be much longer?"

"I don't think so. Perhaps you could talk to me a little?"

"I'd like that," declared the scholar. "Because I'll freely confess to you that I didn't really understand what he was saying over the telephone."

"I was there," declared Chantecoq, "and I felt he was speaking very clearly."

"Doubtless I misunderstood?"

"But I can repeat precisely what he said to you. He said, 'I just found you a new client. Come and meet me at once at

196

the hotel on the Quai d'Orsay. Ask to speak to Master Josset, notary.' That was it, wasn't it?"

"Precisely, monsieur."

"Well then! Your new client is my wife."

"Your wife?"

"Yes, my wife," Chantecoq emphasised. "She cheated on me shamefully."

At those words, a flush of blood turned the scholar's face purple, at the same time as his eyes, involuntarily, instinctively, took on an expression of implacable ferocity.

The king of detectives, who noted all these details carefully, continued in the tone of a man who was truly afflicted by profound sorrow.

"The wretch whom I adored, who was my joy, my whole life, left me, taking off with a hundred thousand francs, to be with her lover. A young interloper, a filthy foreigner she met in a Nantes dancehall. And you know what reason this ragamuffin found to justify her conduct? She claimed that, absorbed by my work, I was neglecting her, I was no longer taking care of her."

Chantecoq didn't continue. The professor had interrupted him with a bestial roar, which drew itself out like the cry of a cruelly injured animal.

Standing, his eyes haggard, bulging from his face, foam on his lips, the scholar rasped, "Where is she? Where is she? I want to kill her, kill her, kill her!"

With one hand, the great bloodhound seized his arm and, with the other, removing his wig and beard, he said, meeting the scholar's eyes, "No more killing, Professor. It's your turn to answer for your actions!"

"Chantecoq!" the scholar recognised him.

And he crashed to the floor, as though he had been

struck by a club.

The king of detectives was about to lean over him. But he heard the sound of muffled footsteps. He turned back: Will Strimer, who had learned the art of getting out of the tightest shackles from the famous Houdini, had slipped his bonds, removed his gag, and was approaching with a knife in his hand, ready to stab his loyal adversary in the back, treacherously.

Chantecoq, fast as lightning, took out his strangely-shaped pistol, of which we spoke earlier and, pointing it at Will's face, just as he was almost upon him, he pulled the trigger.

No gunshot boomed, and yet the American crashed to the floor as though a bullet had torn through his brain.

Chantecoq had just used, once more with success, his famous tranquiliser pistol[14] which he had invented in collaboration with one of our most illustrious chemists and the best gunsmith in Paris, and thanks to which he had already obtained marvellous results, putting to sleep the bandits that he attacked or indeed against those from whom he had to defend himself.

While contemplating his two adversaries, neither one of whom was displaying any sign of life, he muttered to himself.

"With the American, I'm easy. He won't wake until morning. As to the other, he's just fainted and I can restore him in minutes to the reality that awaits him. My work is done. Should I notify Lereni? I've plenty of time, and I admit, without hesitation, I wouldn't mind having a final meeting with the Ladykiller, which would completely establish the degree of his culpability in my mind.

---

[14] This gun is used by the American FBI (Author's footnote)

"To obtain a full, absolute confession from this criminal, the like of whom I've not yet encountered on my journey, wouldn't that add a chapter as unexpected as it would be moving to my numerous adventures? Very well! Let's do it!"

He leaned over the professor. Chantecoq noticed at once that he would not need to use any smelling sales in order to bring him back to consciousness.

Courtil was beginning to stir slightly. Slowly, his eyes opened, revealing a gaze that was vaguely troubled which revealed that, morally, the scholar had not returned to his senses.

Chantecoq stepped away, so that the professor didn't notice his presence straight away. Painfully, the scholar sat up. He seemed dazed. Doubtless a veil was obscuring his vision, because, slowly, with the gestures of an automaton, he rubbed his eyes.

Then he squeezed his forehead with both hands. Several sighs heaved his chest, and the last ended in a sort of painful moan: anguished, expressing his full distress, disarray and perhaps all the remorse that was in him. He kept trying to stand.

Then he noticed, lying around two metres away from him, the American's body. On seeing it, he was transfixed with surprise and dread.

Then, as though he didn't have the strength to stand on his two feet, he crawled towards Will Strimer with a bestial gait, both excited by curiosity and held back through fear.

Chantecoq let him do it. And slipping behind the curtains of one of the two windows, he prepared to observe what was going to happen.

Not without some hesitation, Courtil, whose face was contorted into a worrying rictus, arrived by the American's side. He looked at him for a moment, with a bewildered air, shook his head and, while a little foam appeared at the corners of his mouth, he muttered loud enough that Chantecoq could hear him, "I'm sure I've seen this man somewhere before!"

He grabbed him by the arm and shook him, but Will Strimer, knocked out cold, didn't even make a groan of protest.

Still out loud, the scholar continued, sounding more and more afraid. "He's dead! Why is he dead? Who killed him? Or why was he killed? It wasn't me, no, it wasn't me. And yet, why am I here? And what's this, here?"

He stayed on his knees, near the American's inanimate corpse, leant over him, repeating,

"I've seen him before, but where? How? I don't remember; I don't know; I don't understand."

The king of detectives, who was following this scene with passionate interest from his hiding place, thought, "This man is obviously sincere. So he's not a psychopath, as I thought, or even an irresponsible maniac, but completely mad. Unless, as in the hero of that ever so poignant play, *Procureur Hallers*[15], he has within him a double personality which means that, by turns, he is the most peaceable of men and the most formidable of murderers. Let's make sure of this."

Raising the curtain behind which he was hiding, Chantecoq advanced rapidly towards Professor Courtil, who was staring at him with the eyes of one who was hallucinating.

When he was quite close, he heard him repeating the

---

[15] A reference to the 1893 German play *Der Andere* (*The Other*) by Paul Lindau (1839-1919). It was filmed several times, and one such adaptation came out in 1930, the year *after* this book was published.

same phrases he had just proclaimed a moment before, while looking at Will Strimer. "I've seen him before, but where? How? I don't remember. I don't understand."

Without violence, and even rather gently, the king of detectives took the professor by the arm and, watching him carefully, he said, "Look at me as I'm looking at you and try to remember."

The scholar didn't try to look away.

The expression on his face indicated his state of mind very clearly: profound stupefaction and indecision which was as sincere as it was absolute.

This attitude strangely resembled that of a sleeper, woken suddenly and torn from a nightmare whose details he no longer recalls, but whose morbid influence he continues to suffer.

All this reinforced the thesis that Chantecoq had adopted: a double personality, when he was researching the motives that pushed a man of such great talent, from rigid honesty and fine character, to become the Ladykiller.

Now he was no longer in any doubt: only a violent mental trauma could have split this man into two, but two men unaware of each other, two entirely distinct personalities with no point of comprehension between them, separated into waterproof compartments, which kept them in mutual ignorance, so well that each of them could only become active when completely separated from the other.

Two souls in one body, one an admirable man of genius, of profound virtue; the other, a sadist, a criminal, an implacable executioner: such was the phenomenon that Professor Courtil was displaying!

It appeared to the detective that it was no longer a case of the scaffold or the asylum, where this unfortunate belonged,

201

but to science.

What an extraordinary subject for study he would make, indeed, for his former colleagues. Remembering all the harm they had done him, the great bloodhound ceased thinking about the conclusion of his investigation.

He was wondering if it might not be better to deliver this madman to justice rather than to the examinations of his peers.

Anyway, one last doubt lingered in him: who was to say that he hadn't found himself faced with one of those extraordinary performances, which was seeking to change his mind, to dupe him, to obtain promises and to take the opportunity to escape him, as well as public vindication, which could only be implacable where he was concerned.

Chantecoq was not the kind of man to linger in such uncertainty. He never left anything in the shadows and the case he was about to conclude was one where it was vital to shed light on everything.

He had decided not to put a final stop to it until he had shone a light on his mind, resolved with all the power of his reason, the last proposition of the problem which remained for him to elucidate.

He was still holding the scholar by the arm, and he wasn't trying to disengage from this grip, any more than he was taking his eyes from the bloodhound's.

One would have said, instead, that he was instinctively imploring from him protection against a danger he couldn't see, but which he sensed.

And from his trembling lips, these words escaped, murmured with the accent of a prayer much more than that of a question. "Who are you, monsieur?"

And as Chantecoq didn't answer at once, he articulated,

anxious as a child who feared being punished for a misdemeanour of which he was innocent, "Forgive me for not recognising you. But, at the moment, my memory is like a hole in which there's no longer anything but shadows. I don't remember anything. My thought is incapable of grasping anything but what I have before me. And it's terrifying. I'm like a living corpse who suddenly entered an unknown world or rather like a blind man who suddenly sees daylight again, after long, very long years of darkness.

"Help me, monsieur, to get out of this painful state, tell me, will you help me?"

"Certainly," agreed the king of detectives.

And at once, he asked, "Do you remember your name?"

The scholar thought for a moment, then he shook his head.

"I'll tell you," continued the great bloodhound. "You're called Professor Courtil."

The scholar shuddered, lowered his eyelids, as though he felt the sudden need to shut himself away. For a few seconds, he remained silent, unmoving. Then, still with his eyes closed, he said, "Yes, I'm Professor Courtil."

Chantecoq continued. "You're a great, a very great scholar. Unfortunately, you have been the victim of your colleagues' jealousy, who attempted to bar the route to a man of such genius as they must have been forced to acknowledge in you.

"Your theories were as audacious as they were theoretical, and risked turning upside down the frail scaffold of empiricism on which modern medicine rests, much more perhaps than ancient medicine. They didn't want that. They broke you."

"How well you know me!" the professor sighed. "Yes,

203

that's true: that pack of upstarts stifled me; without that, I would have done great things. But continue reminding me of my life, calling me back to existence, because you've not finished, have you?"

"No, I've not finished," declared Chantecoq, with a grave voice tinged with emotion.

Because he felt the moment of the great test had arrived.

And he spoke, weighing his words and meeting the eyes of the scholar, which for a few seconds had eluded him.

"Armed as you were, you certainly wouldn't have given up the struggle, deserted the battlefield, if the most terrible catastrophe you could have feared hadn't struck you."

"The most terrible catastrophe?" Courtil replied, growing pale.

Chantecoq continued. "You were married to a woman whom you adored."

"What!" the scholar exclaimed, his teeth chattering. "How! You knew that too…"

"And many other things too," affirmed the famous bloodhound, who felt growing from minute to minute the domination that he was already exerting over his quarry.

And, rapping out his words, as if he wanted to make them penetrate more deeply, more directly in his brain which was beginning to resume its state of receptivity, he continued.

"One day, you found proof you had been betrayed."

"Me!" the professor exclaimed, his face clenching with all his renewed sorrow.

"Yes, you," insisted the king of detectives. "So you wanted to punish the culprit yourself. She was your first victim."

A hoarse cry escaped the scholar, who staggered. Chantecoq held him up, and led him to sit on an armchair.

Leaning over him, the bloodhound, who had resolved to see things through to the very end, continued. "You left to take refuge in a cottage in Brittany. Not to flee a justice that you knew very well couldn't touch you, but to distance yourself from a place, from an ambience, which constantly evoked your past happiness and could only add to your present distress. Through work and retirement, you sought peace of mind and you tried to forget.

"You managed this only intermittently. Despite your sincere and worthy efforts, you couldn't chase from your thoughts the memory of she who had betrayed you. It haunted you constantly.

"Soon, you were unable to have a moment's respite. And the continuity of your suffering ended by creating within you a second individual, completely different to the man you had been up to then, a being who was hateful, violent, vindictive, who soon lost all control.

"That's how you came, gradually, to incarnate in your own eyes a kind of crusader, who would give himself the mission of punishing adulterous women. You put all the resources of your scientific genius in the service of that cause; you no longer directed your mind on anything but one sole aim; and you, who had invented a method of reanimating lethargics, you established a chemical formula, with which you put to sleep all the guilty spouses you encountered on your way, or who were brought to your terrible attention.

"You hesitated to make use of that formula for a long time. Your *double* fought against your original personality, that of a great honest man. But one day he became the strongest. The fixed idea took hold of you and you were transformed into a kind of serial killer from which nothing, not even the most basic sense of pity, could now save you.

"However, your conscience prevented you from striking with deadly force. You revolted at the thought of condemning an innocent.

"The proof is that when I demonstrated to you that Madame Barrois wasn't guilty, you didn't hesitate for a moment to reanimate her, to wake her, to save her.

"And yet, at that moment, you were under the influence of your double. You had entirely abdicated your original personality. But this is only a digression; I'll close the brackets and return at once to our subject.

"I told you that you were refusing to strike in error and that you were determined to strike with certainty. And there's how was born in you the idea to talk to one of those shady private detectives, whom you see there and who is more guilty than you, as he was in possession of his free will and complete responsibility. He pointed out those that you needed to sacrifice.

"Who knows if, besides the error I signalled to you myself, there might be others?

"Ah! Professor Courtil, why couldn't you remain yourself? Are you more advanced, now you've obeyed the instinct for destructive vengeance that animates you, now you've littered your path with corpses? Don't you feel remorse gripping you, at the thought of those unfortunates you buried alive in their tombs?

"Didn't you think that, among your victims, there were those who might claim great attenuating circumstances and that many who strayed were soon struck by repentance?

"Did you think that those women had husbands who were unaware of their crime and might perhaps have remained unaware of it forever? Or unaware children, for whom alone, you ought to have held back.

"No, Professor Courtil, the fixed idea dominated you to such a point that you became implacable. I don't doubt for a moment that, each time this vile Strimer showed you a victim, you felt a sadistic joy, an infernal elation.

"Why, at that moment, didn't you hear echoing in your ears the verses of the poet of *Jésus de Nazareth*[16]:

> *Full of pity for the adulterous woman,*
> *Who kneels and weeps in his path,*
> *He says to those who throw the stones:*
> *'On your own heart have you laid a hand?'"*

"Enough, enough," interrupted Professor Courtil, bursting into tears.

The king of detectives let him release all his despair.

The waterproof compartment which had separated the scholar from his double for so many long years, was disintegrating. The process was re-establishing, reconciling, and fusing these two souls that had been strangely separated and hermetically sealed from all contact, into one unique personality.

Before being judged by men, the scholar was judging himself.

The verdict to which he was condemning himself was not long in falling from his lips.

"Monsieur Chantecoq," he said in a grave and calm voice, "I have, thanks to you, returned entirely to my senses. I'll add only one word: a man such as myself must disappear, without delay. Kill me, as you killed Will Strimer."

---

[16] *Jesus of Nazareth,* by Charles Gounod (1818-1893).

Looking towards the inert American, Chantecoq assured him. "I never kill, I sedate. This rogue is plunged into a deep sleep, from which he will wake only in a firmly locked prison cell."

"Then," exclaimed Professor Courtil with terror, "you want to send me to prison?"

And without giving the king of detectives time to answer him, he cried, "I beg you to spare me that shame. Not that I have any fear of punishment. Didn't I just ask you to kill me? No, death doesn't make me tremble; if you knew, instead, how I'm staring it straight in the face! Strike me then and get it over with at once! Kill me!

"You don't want to… Very well! Allow me to bring myself to justice. It must be done, not only to avoid the dreadful trial. No one, other than you, will understand that I acted under the grip of a sort of hypnotic trance from which you've awoken me.

"Don't let any other doctors examine me. They might save me from the guillotine. They will conclude that I acted under diminished responsibility, and it would be prison or, if they believe me to be mad, the asylum. I want neither one nor the other, any more than freedom, because it's frightful to say, but if I remained at liberty, *I would be afraid of starting afresh!*"

"The poor man," thought Chantecoq, "he'll never be cured!"

Shaken by fresh sobs, the professor continued. "Leave me all that I need. It won't take long. Barely a second. But don't look at me like that any more, because as long as your eyes remain fixed on my own, I won't have the strength to make the slightest gesture.

"Your eyes petrify me. It seems to me that my whole

208

body is nothing but a slab of rock, my brain alone is living. My legs, my arms, I can no longer move them. A hundred kilo weight is crushing my chest. I no longer feel anything but a sensation of intense cold, and now that… my tongue… clouds… everywhere… the night… night…"

The scholar's head fell back on the armchair's cushion. Chantecoq leaned over to check his heart was still beating.

It was beating at regular intervals. Chantecoq took the scholar's pulse, it was not that of someone in pain. He pinched his arm hard, but without observing any reflex. His eyes were fixed, but not glassy, resembling two large open windows.

"Paralysed," said the king of detectives, with the assured tone of a doctor sure of his diagnosis.

And he added, "Better it should be this way!"

He went to the telephone. First, he asked for a connection to his own home.

Soon he heard Météor's voice echoing on the other end of the line. "Hello! Is that you, boss?"

"Yes, lad. Everything's fine! Go to bed and sleep in peace. It's all over."

"Boss… I…."

Météor couldn't say anything more. The great bloodhound had already hung up the receiver. Chantecoq waited for a minute or two. Then he asked for Lereni's number. When he had obtained it, he called into the machine.

"Cocorico!"

But this rallying cry didn't have a note of triumph. It was even imprinted with a certain sadness. The king of detectives was thinking, indeed, of all those who paid so dearly for a moment of madness, an hour of folly. He was also thinking

209

about that formidable genius, that great broken man, who could have accomplished such great things and of whom his colleagues' hostility and his wife's infidelity had made one of the most fearsome serial killers who ever lived.

Now the Ladykiller was nothing more than a rag, a wreck, a body without a soul, a soul without a body. Nothing!

If a little life still persisted in him, it was only an already distant echo of past vibrations. It wasn't even an agony, not even the last gleam which was extinguished, but a sort of mechanical survival, such as, it's said, executed criminals experience after their head has been severed.

When Monsieur Lereni finally entered the hotel room where this scene unfolded, he found Chantecoq who was contemplating, with an expression of unspeakable sadness, all that remained of a man of genius.

EPILOGUE

Some days after the events we just described, Chantecoq, sat in his study before his desk, was reading aloud the following article to his secretary and collaborator Météor, which a great daily newspaper had published.

We reproduce this article below in its entirety.

We have already recounted to our readers with what skill Monsieur Lereni, the chief of police, had succeeded, with the aid of his finest inspectors, to discover and arrest the Ladykiller, Professor Courtil, and his accomplice the American private detective Will Strimer.

We also recounted that this arrest took place in a hotel on the left bank where the dreadful and maniacal author of these atrocious massacres was holding a meeting with his henchman.

Let us now complete our report of this matter.

Monsieur Lereni and his inspectors found themselves faced with a man struck by an attack of paralysis and another, who, lying on the ground, appeared dead drunk.

The first was none other than Professor Courtil who, given his state, was immediately sent to the infirmary; as to the second, it was the

American Strimer, who was taken away by agents and locked in a cell where he was kept under close surveillance.

This odious person only awoke at nine o'clock in the morning. At first he had great difficulty gathering his wits, but, skillfully interrogated, he ended up making a full confession and acknowledging that it was indeed he who was indicating to the Ladykiller the unfortunate women that the killer would, a few hours later, strike down with his mysterious poison.

We address our most sincere congratulations to the chief of police, as well as to his agents, and we hope the government will see fit to reward such a magnificent exploit, at their convenience.

Stop Press: We have learned at the last minute that Professor Courtil has succumbed. The American Will Strimer alone will answer to our country's justice for this frightful series of crimes.

While a smile full of bonhomie spread over Chantecoq's face, Météor said,

"Ah well! Boss, all the same, I think they laid it on a bit thick at police headquarters."

"Why, my friend?"

"By Jove! Who succeeded in cracking the case? It was you! I believe, myself, if you hadn't been there, those gentlemen would still be floundering, and how!"

"That's possible," declared the great bloodhound modestly. "But I'm delighted. I had the chance to be of service not only to one of my former pupils, who has become one of my close friends, but also to that institution which is charged with watching over the security of our fellow citizens, the police force, whose admirable efforts there's too great a tendency to disparage."

"Boss, it's almost as though you want to rejoin them."

"No, my dear lad, what would I do there? Certainly no better than those who run it and who, each day, practice with such intelligence and, furthermore, tact, the instrument so delicate to handle that they have on their hands. But what I can still do is lend them my anonymous support, each time they feel the need, and perhaps this will be an opportunity for new and noble adventures for both of us.

"You see, my little Météor, we live in an age where honest people must join together to fight the good fight against the scoundrel. There must be no cliques, no gangs, but a permanent collaboration, direct or indirect, according to circumstances, between all those who are apt, whether by their functions, their knowledge or their habits, to improve the conditions of human existence; in a word, to conduct themselves humanely and honestly under all circumstances."

"Boss," cried Météor, "as always, you're right."

Chantecoq, taking out his pipe, began to fill it with the care he employed every time he carried out this ritual, and, while lighting it, he said,

"Now, I think we can take a good two months of holiday!"

FIN

**CHANTECOQ AND MÉTÉOR RETURN IN
CHANTECOQ AND THE DEVIL'S DAUGHTER!**

ABOUT THE AUTHOR

Arthur Bernède (5 January 1871 – 20 March 1937) was a French writer, poet, opera librettist, and playwright.

Bernède was born in Redon, Ille-et-Vilaine department, in Brittany. In 1919, Bernède joined forces with actor René Navarre, who had played Fantômas in the Louis Feuillade serials, and writer Gaston Leroux, the creator of Rouletabille, to launch the Société des Cinéromans, a production company that would produce films and novels simultaneously. Bernède published almost 200 adventure, mystery, and historical novels. His best-known characters are Belphégor, Judex, Mandrin, Chantecoq, and Vidocq. Bernède also collaborated on plays, poems, and opera libretti with Paul de Choudens; including several operas by Félix Fourdrain.

Bernède also wrote the libretti for a number of operas, among them Jules Massenet's Sapho and Camille Erlanger's L'Aube rouge.

ABOUT THE TRANSLATOR

Andrew Lawston grew up in rural Hampshire, where he later worked for a short time as a French teacher. He moved to London to work in magazine publishing, alongside pursuing his interests in writing, translation, and acting.

In addition to translating the chronicles of Chantecoq for the English-speaking world, Andrew has written a number of science-fiction and urban fantasy books, full of his particular brand of humour. Andrew currently lives in West London with his lovely wife Mel, and a little black cat called Buscemi. There, he cooks curries, enjoys beer and quality cinema, and he dreams of a better world.

ALSO AVAILABLE

CHANTECOQ

Chantecoq and the Aubry Affair
Chantecoq and Wilhelm's Spy I: Made In Germany
Chantecoq and Wilhelm's Spy II: The Enemy Within
Chantecoq and Wilhelm's Spy III: The Day of Reckoning
Chantecoq and the Mystery of the Blue Train
Chantecoq and the Haunted House
Chantecoq and the Aviator's Crime
Chantecoq and Zapata
Chantecoq and the Amorous Ogre
Chantecoq and the Père-Lachaise Ghost
Chantecoq and the Condemned Woman
Chantecoq and the Ladykiller
Chantecoq and the Devil's Daughter

By Andrew Lawston

Detective Daintypaws: A Squirrel in Bohemia
Detective Daintypaws: Buscemi at Christmas
Detective Daintypaws: Murder on the Tesco Express
Zip! Zap! Boing!
Voyage of the Space Bastard
Rudy on Rails

Printed in Great Britain
by Amazon

22624787R00128